MISTED MEMORY

Kirsty Flint finds herself falling in love with the devastatingly attractive Mike Sommerton — but then she learns of the death of Mike's wife Louise in an accident four years previously. As she begins to dig into the past, Kirsty finds herself wondering if Mike is deceiving her. Other disconcerting questions start to niggle at her as well. Why is Mike's son Toby still so disturbed about the past, and why is Mike so reluctant to discuss his wife's death? Could Mike be a wife-killer?

BETH JAMES

MISTED MEMORY

Complete and Unabridged

LINFORD
Leicester

First published in Great Britain

First Linford Edition
published 2014

A catalogue record for this book is available
from the British Library.

ISBN 978–1–4448–2043–0

Published by
F. A. Thorpe (Publishing)
Anstey, Leicestershire

Set by Words & Graphics Ltd.
Anstey, Leicestershire
Printed and bound in Great Britain by
T. J. International Ltd., Padstow, Cornwall

This book is printed on acid-free paper

1

'Well done, Toby! That was great!' With a wide grin spreading across her naturally smiley face, Kirsty clapped her hands in delight as eight-year-old Toby desperately continued his ungainly splash across the width of the pool.

In the course of her job as a fitness and swimming instructor, Kirsty came to know her pupils quite well. Of course, when she took a whole group of children it wasn't quite so easy, but she made it her business to at the very least learn each child's name and just how overly confident or cautious they were when faced with no arm bands and a sheet of turquoise water.

Toby came under the category of 'nervous, but a real trier'. She had taken to him from the off and he, in his turn, had guardedly warmed to her, responding to her cheerful smile and

1

frequent use of his name with a couple of blinks and a quick raise of the hand in an embarrassed half-salute. Kirsty had often had to deny the impulse to ruffle his dark hedgehog-like hair and tell herself firmly: no favourites. But when the group course had finished and she'd received a short, succinct call from Toby's father's personal assistant booking some private lessons, she'd been only too happy to agree.

'Mr Sommerton is delighted with Toby's progress,' said the clipped, efficient voice on the phone. 'In order to consolidate all that Toby's learned so far, he'd like you to take him for a further one-to-one lesson a week in term time, and in the school holidays perhaps two lessons a week, depending on how Toby feels.'

'That would be great,' confirmed Kirsty. 'Toby's a lovely kid and tries very hard, but he lacks confidence, although don't for goodness sake tell him I said that. Private lessons are just the answer. I'm sure we'll both enjoy them.'

So arrangements had been made and, at three thirty every Wednesday, Toby was delivered to the swimming pool by a dark-haired lady in her twenties who, without leaving the car, waved a cheery goodbye as soon as she saw that Kirsty was there waiting for him.

After a shaky start, Toby was now making good progress and Kirsty found herself becoming more and more fond of him. He was bright and polite, and had a way of humming to himself when he thought no one was listening. When swimming was over he sat damp-haired with a hot chocolate from the vending machine. His dark eyes would look at her over the top of the plastic cup and blink in time with the swinging of his foot banging against the table leg. For some reason she found this particularly endearing.

Although Kirsty never questioned her pupils, she was aware that the lady who delivered Toby and came to pick him up after his lesson was not his mother. She was too young for a start, and although

3

Toby referred to his father as Dad, he called her Saskia.

'Hi Tobes,' Saskia would say in her accented English, giving him a high five rather than the kiss Kirsty would expect from a mother. 'Here is my little channel swimmer . . . How many widths today do you manage?' And, with a further smile towards Kirsty, 'His father will be wanting to know.' Kirsty would then give a brief update as to his improvement, confirm the next lesson and wave goodbye with her usual 'See you next week then Toby,' all the time wondering just a little about the whereabouts of his mother.

Today though, was different.

He got changed with his usual speed and, by the time Kirsty caught up with him, was sipping at his chocolate and munching his way through a packet of shortbread biscuits. His hair was still in the main sleekly wet, but on the crown a few springy tufts had leapt back to life. The foot-swinging was in full progress.

4

Saskia was late. At first, Toby seemed not to notice. He was busy watching the exploits of the other swimmers through the plate-glass windows that overlooked the pool. Then, as the pool started to empty, Kirsty watched the realisation slowly creep up on him that certainly by now, Saskia should have appeared to drive him home.

He shot an anxious look in Kirsty's direction. 'D'you think she's had an accident?' he said, but so quietly she hardly heard him.

Quickly she gave a reassuring smile. 'No, of course not! She's either forgotten the time, or there's a hold-up on that roundabout down the road.'

Toby had stopped humming now but the leg swinging continued. 'Accidents do happen, you know,' he informed her as though she had no knowledge of such things. His face had taken on a pinched expression.

Kirsty smiled a confident smile. 'I know they do, Toby, but not very often; and in my experience when someone's

5

a little late to collect a pupil, there's a very simple explanation.'

Toby took a moment to digest this. He kicked the table leg as he shifted in his seat. 'What sort of explanation?'

'Well,' said Kirsty, 'it could be that the television's on and they're so engrossed in the programme they just forget the time. Or sometimes there's a traffic jam.'

'She doesn't watch television very much, and she puts the buzzer on the cooker thing for when she has to leave. My dad told her to do it so she can't forget. Anyway, Saskia's very reliable because we need someone reliable in our lives, my dad said.'

Oh did he? thought Kirsty.

Toby twisted his chair round a bit further so he could watch along the corridor to the glass automatic doors that led to the car park for swimmers. He looked serious. Far too serious for an eight-year-old.

'Tell you the funniest thing that stopped someone turning up on time, shall I?' asked Kirsty, wanting Toby to look more like a child and less like an anxious adult. Interested, Toby eyed her enquiringly. 'This lady — her name was Michelle — well, she used to always come and pick up her daughter after her lesson and, same as you, her daughter was never kept waiting,' started Kirsty, wondering how long she could spin the story out. 'Well, we were sat here waiting and waiting — much, much longer than we've been waiting today, Toby. And do you know what had happened?' Toby shook his head but his eyes had wandered back to the door as though willing Saskia to appear. 'Well, Michelle was just leaving the house when she realised she needed to visit the downstairs cloakroom before she left. She knew she was pushed for time, so she was rushing a bit. She heard a bit of a clink and thought it was the blind tapping against the cloakroom window so she didn't take a lot of notice. She flushed the loo, washed her hands, shut the door and looked for her keys

7

because she was sure she'd had them in her hand earlier.' Kirsty paused. Toby looked at her expectantly.

'Her keys weren't on the hall table where she thought they might be. But then she saw that she'd left the front door slightly open and she remembered that she'd actually gone out to the car before deciding she should visit the loo, so she thought to herself that that was alright then, she must have left the keys in the car. So . . . '

'So?' repeated Toby.

'So, she went out to the car, the house door slammed behind her and she found that she hadn't even unlocked the car, and the keys were nowhere to be seen!'

'So, she couldn't get into her house or her car then?' said Toby after a moment's contemplation.

'Right,' said Kirsty.

'So what did she do?'

'Well, she didn't have her phone with her either, her neighbour wasn't in, and her husband hadn't got home from work yet.'

'Oh,' said Toby. 'So she was locked out and couldn't tell anyone?'

'Right,' said Kirsty again. 'But mothers, you know, can be very enterprising.'

'Enterprising?'

'Think their way round things. Michelle walked round the side of the house to where the small cloakroom window was, and luckily she'd left it on the catch.'

'On the catch?'

'Slightly open. But it was quite high off the ground so she looked round for something to stand on and saw the dustbin. She lifted the dustbin to under the window, hauled herself onto it . . . Did I mention it was winter time?'

'No,' said Toby, his eyes on her face. 'So it was dark then.'

'You've got it exactly. By this time she couldn't really see what she was doing, but she was desperate to get to her keys or her phone, or anything really.'

'She fell in the dustbin, didn't she?'

'No, she didn't. She might have done

9

though, come to think of it,' said Kirsty, relieved to see that she'd raised a bit of a smile and at least taken his mind off Saskia's non-appearance. 'Eventually she managed to get the window further open, but it wasn't a very big window. It was a struggle, but somehow she managed to wriggle her shoulders through and get a grip on the inside sill. She pushed her feet against the dustbin, hoping to give herself the lift she needed, but as she pushed against the dustbin it toppled over, leaving her half inside and half outside the window with her legs hanging in the air . . . '

Horrified, Toby looked at her. Hoping she hadn't made a terrible mistake — because usually by now she was raising a wide grin, if not a hoot of laughter — Kirsty smiled and reached across the table to put her hand over his. He snatched at away as though he'd been burned. Goodness, he was a nervous child!

'It's all right, Toby. There's a happy ending, I promise.' She took a breath and continued. 'For the moment, poor

Michelle was completely stuck. She tried in vain to move herself either in, or out, of the window — by this time she didn't care which, so long as she could get free . . . Then, just when she thought she could bear it no longer, there was a screech of brakes and a car drew up in her drive.' She lowered her voice to make it sound mysterious. 'Heavy footsteps started to come down the side of the dark house towards her. She knew they weren't her husband's footsteps . . . Who could it be? She stopped struggling and kept very still.'

Toby's eyes were like saucers. 'What happened?'

'A voice said, 'Allo, allo, allo. What's going on 'ere then? We've had a report that someone's attempting to break in . . . Is this *your* house, madam?' And Michelle felt someone pulling her leg.'

'Pulling her leg?'

'Yes. Just like I'm pulling yours now!' Kirsty grinned.

Toby didn't grin back. 'I don't understand?'

Oh dear, why had she ever started on this story? 'OK, Toby. Don't look so worried. What happened was — a lady living across the street, who Michelle hardly knew, had seen someone down the side of the house and not realising or expecting it to be Michelle breaking into her own house, thought it was a burglar and called the police. The police came round, managed to help Michelle back through the window and phoned the swimming pool. Of course I stayed on a while with her daughter, and I phoned Michelle's husband, who came and picked up the daughter on his way home from work. And every one lived happily ever after. OK?'

Toby thought for a few seconds. 'Where were the keys then?'

'Well, that's the really funny part. The keys had fallen down the toilet and Michelle had flushed them just out of sight round the bend, so they didn't find them straight away.'

Once again Toby looked horrified. 'So someone had to put their hand down the toilet to get them out?' He chewed that one over, then, for the first time, there was a glimmer of a smile. 'How gross!' He gave a sudden gurgle of laughter and Kirsty found herself laughing too.

'It really *is* a true story,' she said, even though he was still laughing. 'I just couldn't resist the bit about me pulling your leg. Pulling your leg means when you're having someone on.'

'Eh?' said Toby.

Oh dear, this was hard. 'Having a joke with them. Oh, you must know what I mean.'

'No I don't,' said Toby blinking hard.

Could this child really have lived for eight years without understanding what a joke was? 'Come on, Toby. You must do!'

Suddenly a dimple appeared in his cheek and she caught a glimpse of shy cheeky humour in his eye. 'You mean like I am with you, now?' He collapsed on the table with mirth.

So, he had a sense of humour after

all. Kirsty gave a relieved chuckle and wondered what other stories she could dig up from her limited repertoire of funny stories suitable for eight-year-olds, when she became aware that the outside door was opening. She looked up to see a silver-haired man walking purposefully towards them.

Oh great, Toby's grandfather had come to collect him.

'Oh, here's my dad,' said Toby, still with a grin on his face.

The smile on Kirsty's lips froze slightly. That had been a close one. She'd been on the point of saying, 'I expect you've come for your grandson.' How embarrassing would that have been? Now he'd come closer, she could see that of course he was much too young to be Toby's grandfather; for, despite the thick grey distinguished-looking hair and a brooding manner that added years to his persona, Toby's father had the clean-cut good looks of a man in his mid- to late-thirties. Actually, apart from his eyes, which were a light greeny grey, he bore a passing resemblance to George Clooney on one of his more serious days.

'I'm so sorry,' he said now. 'Saskia rang me to let me know the car wouldn't start and I asked her to ring the pool before coming myself to collect Tobes. I take it the message was passed on? I do hope we haven't put you out by keeping you late.'

'No big deal,' said Kirsty with a friendly smile which belied the sudden dryness of her throat and the steady but loud beating of her heart. 'Toby and I have been telling each other stories. The time went quite fast.'

'Well, thank you anyway. Thank you very much. Oh, um, sorry — I can't think of your name for the minute . . . '

Ah, now he smiled. Just a small smile, but oh, so full of promise. She'd like to see it become much wider; an all-encompassing smile. One that threatened to split his face in half. She thought it would suit him.

'It's Kirsty,' said Toby, looking from

one to the other of them. 'I *told* you it was Kirsty.'

Toby's father ruffled his son's hair with a careless hand. Toby didn't cringe away this time, she noticed. That was a relief anyway. 'So you did,' he said. 'How did you get on, anyway?'

'Good.'

'Improving all the time,' said Kirsty. 'Plenty of practice and he'll turn out to be a strong swimmer.'

Mr Sommerton — for Kirsty had remembered his name too, now — nodded shortly. 'Good, good. That's the idea. Make him into a strong, confident swimmer. Stand him in good stead for the future.'

'Why? Thinking of the Olympics, are you? Or a holiday on a yacht, maybe?' Kirsty kept her tone light and was surprised by the keenness of his return glance.

'It's important to do things well. I believe in giving Toby every chance in life, every opportunity to do well.'

'Of course,' said Kirsty. 'But let's not

forget swimming is a lot of fun too! Especially when you're only eight years old.'

Mr Sommerton turned his attention back to Toby, who had picked up his swimming bag and was hopping from one foot to the other. 'Got everything then? Well, we'd better be off, eh Toby? Thanks again for staying on to keep an eye on him. I appreciate it. I'm sure the pool staff would have obliged, though; he could have sat in the office or something.'

'No trouble,' replied Kirsty, thinking she wouldn't bother to tell him that the message that he was on his way had never got to them and that actually Toby had been quite worried about being picked up. She was sure that when he spoke to Toby he'd find that out. *If* he spoke to Toby, that was. For somehow she had picked up the idea that things were run on very Spartan lines in the Sommerton household, with not too much emphasis placed on fun and good times. She hoped she was wrong but somehow had the feeling she was not.

'Oh, by the way, um, Kirsty. My name's Michael. Mike Sommerton. I'd better give you my card so you can ring me in case anything of this nature should happen again.' As he pressed a business card into her hand, Kirsty felt a small shock from his fingertips as they brushed hers. Unable to stop herself, her eyes flew to his face. He looked as startled as she did.

Quickly she pulled herself together. 'Right, thanks.' She pocketed the card. 'Bye, Toby. No climbing in and out of windows now. You never know when you might get stuck!'

Toby grinned and gave her one of his special salutes.

'What was that all about?' she heard Mike questioning him as they walked ahead of her towards the doors. 'You haven't been climbing in and out of windows, have you?'

'Course not,' Toby said scornfully. 'She was pulling my leg.'

★ ★ ★

Toby got into the back of the car. He was still smiling to himself. Despite her mad hair, which was blonde, sometimes with a pink streak — and on one memorable occasion, a rather amazing shade of turquoise all over — Kirsty was nice; he liked her. For one thing, she was always smiling. For another thing, she never asked him questions he didn't know how to answer. Like, 'What did you do at school today?' or 'What did you have for lunch?' As if he could remember. Anyway, why would anyone want to know?

Kirsty just smiled a lot, and made a game of learning to swim. She seemed to understand that not all boys liked to get their faces splashed, and that he really hated doing duck dives even though he pretended he didn't mind them, because he'd noticed she didn't suggest they do them very often. She'd taught him about the breathing too, so that his arms and legs seemed to work better together and he didn't get that panicky feeling anymore when he was halfway across the pool and felt his breath might run out.

It wasn't that he hated swimming. It was more that there was something connected to the whole idea of being in the water that made him short of breath and confused. He knew that once upon a time he'd loved the idea of splashing around in the shallows on the beach with his dad and his mum.

But now there was just Dad — no Mum.

No Mum to hold his hand. No Mum to whisper in his ear that it was all right because she was there. Because she wasn't anymore, was she? And she wouldn't be again, because that had been explained to him. Grandma and Auntie Sam had said that Mum was in heaven and would always watch over him, but he wasn't too sure he liked that idea. Suppose she was watching him when he was naughty? When he was asked a question he didn't want to answer and he pretended he didn't hear? Suppose she knew when sometimes he got really angry and wanted to punch anyone who asked him one more time if he was all right?

He'd asked his dad once if he thought Mum was watching them. Dad had looked away and spent a lot of time folding up a paper napkin that would be thrown away anyway. 'It's a nice idea, Toby,' he'd said at last. 'And if it helps to think that, there's no one to tell you any different. The truth is, nobody knows.' Then he'd taken hold of Toby's hand. 'Your mum loved us both, Toby. She always knew we'd look out for each other. You and me, mate, we're a team, aren't we?'

And Toby had said yes, because he liked the idea of him and his dad being a team, even if it was only a team of two. Toby had been four then, nearly five. Now at eight, he realised that lots of children were on a team of two and he'd got used to the idea. Just some-times he fancied he'd caught a smell, or heard a laugh that rang a distant memory, and he felt that 'something missing' feeling like a sudden stitch in his side. And then there were the other times when he felt he had to just screw his eyes up very tight so as not to think about something. What the something was, he wasn't sure of, just that he was not on any account to think of it, so he thought about something else instead, like the way he was going to teach Buddy how to roll over and over and maybe jump through a hoop. Although it wouldn't be a hoop that was on fire, because that would be cruel.

At first Grandma had spent a lot of time with him and Dad. Grandma had a way of looking at you as though she knew exactly what was going on in your mind. She was strict over table manners and bedtimes, but would occasionally surprise him with exactly the right present, and she understood there were times when he liked to be alone. She didn't kiss him too much either. Somehow she seemed to know that for boys Mum-kisses were all right, but other kisses weren't really. She'd bought him a puppy too. Well, she said he was hers, but really Toby knew she'd bought him with him in mind. 'When you come here, he can be your buddy. What do you think would be a good name for him?' she'd asked.

Toby had looked at the bright dark doggy eyes peering at him from under a fringe of black and white hair. 'I think Buddy would be,' he'd replied without hesitation.

So although Buddy lived with Grandma because, as Dad reminded him, Grandma was all alone in her bungalow apart from the puppy, Toby knew that Buddy was really his and just on loan to Grandma.

Dad's sister Auntie Sam would sometimes come and visit too, and when she did the house became noisier and untidier, with music playing, shoes left on the stairs, the smell of perfume in the air and more talking and laughing than usual. When Toby asked her why she couldn't live with them all the time, she laughed and said they'd all drive each other nuts within a week, and that anyway as an actress she had to be where the work was and that meant London, not the New Forest, but she loved her 'little breaks' with them.

Sometimes the 'little breaks' coincided with the holiday they took every year at the seaside house on the Devon coast. This was something they had always done since Toby could remember. It was Dad's family's house, left to him by a great aunt. Louise, Toby's mum, had loved it. Toby could remember going for walks with her on the beach, finding shells, watching the waves ripple up higher and higher until they reached his toes and then rush back again, making the skin under the soles of his feet feel strange and unsteady. The same crowd of people were there every year — friends that Louise and Mike had had since long before Toby was born. There were Tracey and Tim with their three children, and Jack and Nina who didn't have any children and for some reason couldn't have them. When he'd asked Mum why not, she had told him he must never, ever, ask Nina the same question as she might be upset. So Toby hadn't, although he'd never felt quite comfortable with Nina, who'd been Mum's best friend since they were girls, because she looked at him a funny way and was always calling him cute, and he wished she wouldn't. He liked Tracy and Tim better because they didn't stare at him all the time and just treated him the same as they did their own kids.

But the holiday in Devon was always good, even if it rained, which it often did. Especially that awful year. The year when he was four and Mum had died . . . But even after that, they all still went — every summer.

'Oh Michael, d'you think it's wise?' Toby remembered hearing Grandma ask, when she first heard of them going the year after Mum's death.

'I've thought about it long and hard, believe me,' Dad had replied in his new patient voice, which meant there was to be no argument. 'Toby needs continuity in his life. There are many happy memories that we all shared there, and . . . ' He took a long pause, and Toby wondered if when he spoke again his voice would be all right or have that wobble to it that Toby dreaded. 'We'll make some more good memories . . . ' It was all right — Dad's voice was strong and steady — but then there was another pause. 'It's no good running away. You can't alter things just by avoiding them. No, it'll be strange without Louise, heaven knows. But she would want it, I'm sure she would.'

So they'd gone to the seaside house and had a sunny holiday. Nina and Jack didn't come that year though. Toby had never found out why, just been glad he hadn't had to put up with the staring. But their other friends had been there, so Toby had children of around his own age and that he'd known from before, to play with — Jenny, Brad, and Rosie, who were the children of Tracey and Tim, to chase the waves with. But it wasn't the same collecting shells without Mum. Auntie Sam helped him sort them out, but she didn't hold them to the light or put them in order of favourites or size.

In the back of the car, Toby thought about whether at eight he was actually too old now to be collecting shells, and then about the next time they'd go to Devon. It would be in the summer holidays, he knew that, but it seemed a long way away. For a brief moment he pictured himself swimming a strong crawl along the beach; then, perched on a surfboard, riding the waves, while on the shore line crowds gathered in admiration and he could hear Dad saying, 'That's my son. He's a very strong swimmer now you know!'

Toby blinked as he felt the car swing into the driveway of their home. Saskia was at the open door. 'Ah, my little channel swimmer, he has returned,' she said in her accented English. 'And what did you have for lunch today?'

Toby sighed.

2

'Hello, Tiger. Did you think I was never coming?'

Kirsty let herself in through the front door of her tiny flat and nearly tripped over a deeply striped ginger cat that started up a purr like an engine and rubbed his ears against her sports shoes.

'Yeah, yeah, yeah. I know I'm late,' she said. 'But I'm here now, aren't I? I'll get your dinner in a moment.'

She opened her sports bag, put her working clothes into the washing machine on top of some towels and switched the machine to gentle wash. Only then did she turn her attention to Tiger, opening a tin of cat food and refreshing the water in his bowl. Before checking on what the fridge had to offer, she stood and watched for a moment as Tiger delicately helped himself to his food. No problem there then. He didn't have to think about what he would eat every evening; he didn't have to trust to luck that his filled plate would be put before him.

Contemplating the meagre contents of the fridge, Kirsty gave a small sigh. She didn't mind living on her own, really; it was just that sometimes it would be nice to come home and find that, regarding supper, someone else had made the decision as to what was on the menu.

Once she'd consumed a quick supper of pasta and a bottled sauce spiced up with some chopped bacon and onions, she felt better and looked round her small ground floor flat with something approaching contentment.

* * *

Kirsty remembered the pride she'd felt when she'd finally closed the door on the removal men and looked round the small space filled with cardboard boxes and furniture that was hardly state-of-the-art, but all hers. That had been two years ago, and despite her mother's misgivings that she would be infinitely better off at home, and her father and brothers' united opinion that she was too much of an airhead to manage alone, she was still here and fiercely proud of her independence.

The move had done her good. Despite her love for her family — and she did love them and had lived with them far too long, she acknowledged to herself — at the family home she'd felt a lesser person. In the large, old, untidy home of her childhood she felt everything she did was examined under a microscope. It was good that at last she could afford a small flat and the liberty to make her own mistakes.

Her mother was a teacher, her father a solicitor, and her brother did something important in the city to do with finance and pensions. And that left Kirsty, who had been the despair of most of her teachers because maths was a mystery and she couldn't spell for toffee — indeed, on a bad day she couldn't even spell 'toffee'. She still found her times tables to be a real challenge, only luckily now she had discovered that computers had a spell check and that texting and using the calculator on her mobile phone did not require a degree.

And she could run, she could swim and she could teach people how to work out. Even the most uncoordinated of people could come to Kirsty for help. She didn't worry if they were over-weight, self-conscious, or went to the right instead of the left. As she often told them during her workouts, 'As long as you're moving, anything will do.' Slowly she'd built up a programme of diverse classes, which meant that her week was filled with doing the two things she liked best — exercise and being friendly to people.

On the whole, Wednesdays were good: a double stretch-and-tone class first thing, followed by water aerobics at twelve, pilates after lunch, then Toby's private lesson at three thirty. A good day; not too hectic, not too much in the way of traveling, and nicely spaced out. Normally by the end of it she was ready to do a few chores and prepare for frenetic Thursday, which left little time for lunch and frequently found her with a sore throat from trying to make herself heard during her lesson for junior swimmers. After that, with nothing else in the offing, she usually turned on the television for some relaxed evening viewing.

Only somehow, this Wednesday evening, she was restless. She was almost relieved when, halfway through a soap whose story line she didn't much care for, her phone rang.

'Hello?'

'Er, Kirsty?' It was a man's voice. Deep and slightly hesitant.

Kirsty's heart started beating a little faster. 'Yes, that's me.'

'Hi! It's Mike . . . Toby's dad.'

She sat up straighter. 'Right.'

'Sorry. Are you busy?'

Was she busy? She used the remote to turn down the sound on the TV. 'Well, no, not really.'

'I just wanted to thank you again for keeping an eye on Toby. It was very good of you. It must have been a good half an hour later than he's normally picked up and, Toby tells me, my message was never passed on to you.'

Kirsty swallowed, telling herself not to be ridiculous, her throat could not possibly be dry as she'd not long ago had a glass of water. 'No it wasn't, but that's OK. As I said before, Toby's no trouble, no trouble at all.'

There was a pause as though perhaps he didn't know what to say next. 'Good, good. Well, I wouldn't expect him to be, really, but all the same I appreciate it. Um, I wouldn't like you to think I'd been offhand when I finally arrived . . . I'd just been rushing a bit to get there and I suppose I was feeling a bit, well . . . ' Mike's words trailed off. He obviously felt he'd been a bit abrupt. Kirsty grinned, wondering whether to risk telling him 'terse' was the word he'd been looking for. Then he took the wind from her sails by saying in an altogether different voice: 'I — I don't like being late for Toby.'

For a moment he sounded almost vulnerable. 'Of course not,' said Kirsty quickly. 'I quite understand. Some kids worry more than others.'

Mike gave a small cough. 'Oh, I don't think he'd *worry*, not really. He knows either Saskia or I will be there eventually.'

'I'm sure,' said Kirsty, recognising that he was trying to tell her that he was a good parent and had everything under control, but wanted to give thanks where thanks were due. And now he had, so goodbye Kirsty Flint. Well, it was nice of him to ring anyway. She got ready to click off.

'Um, he's getting on all right, is he? Toby?'

There it was — that vulnerable note in his voice again. Her heart melted just a little. 'Yes, very well. Not too keen on water in his face still, but I'm sure he'll soon get used to it. And he certainly has tenacity. Won't give up.'

Mike gave another small cough. 'Good. So it's all heading in the right direction then? He used to be quite at home in the water; it's only these last few years that he's been less confident.'

'Maybe someone pushed him in one day, when he wasn't expecting it. It's surprising how often that happens. Sometimes it puts kids off for life.'

'No, it wasn't that,' said Mike.

'Oh?'

'Well, perhaps we'll discuss it some time, but you've got things to do now I expect, and I have to supervise bedtime.'

'OK then. I'll see Toby next week.'

'Yes, and thanks again, er, Kirsty.'

There was a click. Phone conversation finished. Kirsty wondered what he was thinking now. Perhaps she was one more item to be crossed off his list: Phone swimming instructor and explain that Toby is not a neglected child, that it was most unusual for anything as untoward as a late pickup to happen in the Sommerton household.

Well, he'd explained that all right. Kirsty smiled to herself and turned up the volume in an effort to engender interest in the soap and stop brooding about a very uptight silver-haired man who, despite his good body — for naturally, being a fitness instructor, she recognised these things immediately — looked as though he could do with a good laugh; and, by the way, seemed to think her name was 'er, Kirsty.' She wondered if he called Saskia 'er, Saskia', or was it just the letter 'K' he had a problem with? Then she told herself that it was none of her business what he called Saskia or what his relationship was with her, because that was what she'd really been wondering about.

And she ought to stop wondering about it immediately.

The next few weeks passed uneventfully. Saskia arrived cheerfully and promptly to pick Toby up after his lessons. Covertly, Kirsty would examine her during the quick handover, trying to imagine her as Mike's live-in lover. She wouldn't have put them down as a couple, but there was no telling these days. The few words that passed between Saskia and herself were concerned with Toby's headway in the pool. No clues to be picked up there. Saskia asked the question and Kirsty could inform her truthfully that his progress was good.

Finally Toby had learned to relax more completely in the water and frequently demanded jokes, as he called the one-liners that Kirsty, purely in order to watch his delight as the penny dropped, fed him on a regular basis. He'd give a lopsided grin and say that he'd try the jokes out on Dad or Saskia, although she of course wouldn't always understand because of the language. By now Kirsty had figured out that Dad, Grandma Sommerton, Saskia, and Buddy the dog were the constants in Toby's life. He also had a school-friend called Jake who could already swim like a fish, and an aunty called Sam, who was fun. 'A bit like you,' he'd said, which Kirsty took to be a compliment and felt inordinately pleased about.

The lessons were booked in blocks of six. Sometimes Kirsty wondered if the next block of six would happen or whether she'd be notified by Mike Sommerton's P.A. that Toby no longer required lessons, and she'd have to consult her waiting list of pupils for a Wednesday replacement. She didn't look forward to that day at all. There was something about Toby and, to be honest, Toby's dad, that had got under her skin.

Then: 'My dad's picking me up tonight,' said Toby after he came out of the changing rooms one Wednesday at the beginning of June.

'OK. Will he be a bit late then?' asked Kirsty, who was checking her phone for messages.

'He'll try not to be. Saskia's had to go home suddenly. Her mother's ill.'

'Oh dear,' said Kirsty.

'It's all right,' said Toby. 'She'll probably get better. It's nothing life-threatening.'

'Glad to hear it,' said Kirsty wondering what a phrase like 'life-threatening' was doing in the vocabulary of an eight-year-old. Together they stood and watched as Toby's hot chocolate was delivered into its cup. Then they went and sat at the same table as they always did while waiting for Toby to be picked up.

'What it means is,' went on Toby, 'Grandma and Buddy will come and stay, which is good. Well, mainly good, but she's a bit strict sometimes.'

'Right,' said Kirsty, thinking that it seemed Toby's mother was simply never on the scene. Perhaps she'd run off with a Spanish Count or something.

'Well, not all the time. But bedtimes, and eating at the table, and things . . . '

'I understand.'

'Anyway. We don't know when she's coming back, which is a nuisance because Grandma can't stay indefinitely, can she? She's got her life to live, after all. That's what Dad said when I asked him why not.'

'Oh.' Kirsty was still itching to ask about his mother, but of course that wouldn't be professional.

'So we'll just have to see how long it goes on for. We might have to get another if Saskia doesn't come back.'

'What d'you mean, another?'

'Another helper, another or pear,' explained Toby as though Kirsty wasn't really very bright.

'Oh, an *'au pair'*?'

'That's what I said.' Toby gave the table a kick. 'I like Saskia though. She's better than the other one we had. *She* kept crying all the time and she wanted to marry my dad. How gross was that? She had to go in the end. She was driving us both nuts . . . ' He looked up at Kirsty and blinked. 'But Saskia's alright. She already has a boyfriend in

41

Poland, but she needs the work here to save money so they can get married. It's difficult in Poland you know.'

Difficult in England too, thought Kirsty, especially if you didn't have a boyfriend.

'Anyway,' went on Toby, 'my dad's had a special little studio flat done over the garage for or pears, so we all know where the boundaries are.' His eyes blinked again and a sudden grin split his face. 'Here's Dad.'

Goodness, all at once Kirsty found herself hoping her hair looked all right and that her waterproof mascara hadn't smudged, and that well, she just hoped . . .

'Hi, Tobes. Hello, er, Kirsty,' said Mike.

Wow. Since she'd last met him, Mike Sommerton had picked up a slight tan. It made his eyes seem if not exactly green, then less grey and altogether livelier. He was wearing a dark blue sweater and jeans and a small smile which made Kirsty's heart beat a shade faster.

'Oh, hi, um, Mike,' said Kirsty, feeling hot and flustered.

'Not so late this time.'

'No, not so late.' She glanced at her watch. 'Early, in fact!'

'Can we have fish and chips?' said Toby.

'Don't see why not,' said Mike. 'We'll take them home, shall we, and eat them in front of the telly?'

'Grandma's coming tomorrow so we'll have to eat proper food at the table then,' explained Toby to Kirsty.

'Fish and chips are extremely nutritious. Nothing wrong with fish and chips,' said Mike.

'Nothing at all,' said Kirsty. 'Wouldn't mind some myself.'

'Can't she come with us?' Toby asked Mike. 'She's good at telling jokes. You'd like her.'

There was a short, embarrassed silence. 'Sorry.' Mike pulled his ear and sheepishly turned towards Kirsty. 'Kirsty's been working, Tobes. She wants to get home. She's probably got her evening planned.'

43

No, Kirsty wanted to say. *No, I haven't. I'd love to share your fish and chips.*

'That's OK,' she said instead. 'I'll see you next week, Toby . . . Oh, pickup time the same?'

Mike pulled his ear again. 'I'd better ring you. It might be my mother, or me, or possibly Saskia. I'll let you know. Say thanks to Kirsty, Tobes.'

'Thanks, Kirsty,' said Toby obediently. 'If I find any more jokes I'll try and remember.'

With a curious feeling of loss, Kirsty could only stand and watch as the two of them walked away from her.

★ ★ ★

Toby was dreaming.

He was walking along a path. The path was stony he didn't know where he was and he was crying. Something must be very wrong, because he didn't cry for nothing. Someone somewhere was watching him too. He wasn't sure if it was his mum, so he turned round to look for

44

her, but she wasn't there. He'd known she wouldn't be somehow, so he turned back again and went on walking without knowing where he was going. Walking and walking, and he was all alone. He screwed up his face. It was getting very difficult to walk properly; something was making his legs feel as though they were frozen to the ground. And all the time he knew he had to get somewhere; he had to get away. But when your legs won't work there's nothing you can do.

He opened his mouth, trying to call out. But then there was no sound. He couldn't walk, and he couldn't speak!

It was terrible. He was having a terrible time. Where was everyone?

'Wake up, Tobes! It's all right, I'm here, everything's fine.'

Toby's heavy eyelids struggled open and his father's anxious face shimmered into focus. 'I'm all right,' he said immediately.

'I know you are. It was just a bad dream . . . But don't worry, I'll sit here with you till you go back to sleep.'

'I'm all right,' said Toby again.

Dad kissed his cheek. 'More than all right. You're great.'

Toby felt better now. His breathing was easier and he'd forgotten whatever it was he'd been dreaming about. He turned over. 'I thought I couldn't move,' he said.

'That's horrible, Tobes, but you can, you see. It was only a dream.'

'Dad?'

Dad straightened the bedclothes. 'Yes?'

'Why couldn't she come?'

'Who?'

'Kirsty. She's so nice.'

Dad sighed and sat back on the bed. 'Yes, I like her too. But she has her own life.'

'You always say that.'

'Well, only because it's true.'

'She hasn't got a boyfriend.'

'How d'you know that?'

'Because I asked her.'

'Tobes, that's a bit out of order.'

'She didn't mind. She just said, 'No, too much like hard work.' That's all.

She wasn't cross. She's never cross. She would have liked to have fish and chips with us, I know she would.'

Dad looked down at him. 'Well then, perhaps another time, if it presents itself,' he said, which in Toby's book was the same as saying, 'We'll see,' and everyone knew that meant 'no'.

'Right,' said Toby.

Dad was still sitting there. Toby brightened. 'You know, we were going to make a pond?'

Dad sighed again. 'Yes, Tobes.'

'Could we start soon? Spring or summer's the best time for building ponds,' went on Toby relentlessly. 'My teacher said so.'

'I'll think about it,' said Dad.

'Yeah, right.' Toby hunched his back.

'Toby, I said I'd think about it and I will. We have to decide what kind of pond, how big it will be and where to put it. Ponds aren't built in a day, you know . . . '

Toby held his breath. 'It's Whitsun soon and we get a week off.'

'Sounds good to me,' said Dad. 'Now settle down and go to sleep. I promise I'll stay here until you do.'

'Yes, Dad,' said Toby, closing his eyes and snuggling under the covers to hide his grin.

* * *

Kirsty wasn't a great shopper. As a rule, she did two shops a week for food and always used the same sports shops for her working gear of T-shirts, sports pants and shoes. She wasn't fussy about their colour as long as it was bright. Tonight, as she browsed along the almost empty aisles of the supermarket, she was wearing purple sports pants, a cyclamen T-shirt and an orange fleece. Her hair was blonde, but with — this week — a streak of pink running down one side. She thought she looked interestingly funky.

She paused in front of the avocados. They were on special. Gingerly, she felt the top of one of them. Felt about right, so why on special? Had they been stored too cold or too long, and would they prove to be a disappointing brown inside and taste of nothing? She decided to live dangerously and take one. She added it to the basket to sit beside the four tomatoes, lettuce and bag of new potatoes that sat there screaming 'rations for one' to anyone who might be interested enough to look.

'Hello,' said a voice to her right. 'I thought it might be you, er, Kirsty.'

Kirsty felt her face heat up in a way which was sure to clash with the pink hair and orange fleece. 'Oh sorry, you made me jump. I was miles away.'

He was wearing the dark blue sweater again. It suited him, even if it was a bit boring. 'Hello,' he said again.

'Um,' said Kirsty. 'Hello. Um, where's Toby?'

'At home with his Grandma. Hopefully he's done his homework and will be ready for bed by the time I get home. Had a late client tonight so — late home.'

'Client?' asked Kirsty, thinking he surely couldn't be a hairdresser, and who on earth else talked about clients — especially late ones? Perhaps he was a solicitor; then she thought of her father. No, she was sure he wasn't a solicitor. Solicitors didn't have P.A.s, or wear jeans.

'I do kitchens,' he said. 'Quite often I have to see clients in the evenings.'

'Oh I see. Sorry, I wasn't being nosey.'

'Of course not.'

There was a silence that two more approaching shoppers, who looked dolefully at a pile of imported beans, chose not to break.

'Shopping's a bit of a pain, isn't it? I'm afraid I usually leave it to Saskia. She knows all the things Tobes likes but of course she's not here and we've run out of his usual cereal.'

'Ah, and I thought you were stalking me.' It was like watching Toby all over again as a slow smile dawned across Mike's features, and she felt the same momentary glow of triumph that she did every time she raised a smile from

Toby. 'Well, I don't want to stop you,' she said. 'You probably want to get home.'

'Yes,' agreed Mike. 'Good night, then.'

'Good night,' said Kirsty. She finished in the vegetable section and found herself in the meat aisle. While stood looking at the chicken her brain, for some reason, had trouble recognising that it was indeed chicken, not lamb or beef. Out of the corner of her eye she could see Mike contemplating a rack of milk as though trying to decide which of the identical bottles to choose.

'We mustn't keep meeting like this,' she couldn't resist saying as she went past.

He smiled the smile that Kirsty found so endearing on his son, only on Mike it made her heart hammer and her palms sweat a little bit. 'I've nearly finished,' he said.

'Oh,' said Kirsty. Then, because she couldn't think of anything else to say: 'Toby OK for tomorrow?'

'Yes, sure.' He swung round to face

her, holding his wire basket in front of him like a barrier. 'It might be my mother who'll pick him up. She goes to a Women's Institute meeting though, so she'll have to cut that short.'

'That's a shame . . . Look, Toby's my last pupil on a Wednesday. Can't I run him home? It's Vicarage Mount, isn't it?'

Mike looked surprised. 'How d'you know that?'

Kirsty gave an offhand shrug just as though she knew all her pupils' addresses. 'Toby told me. Vicarage Mount's on my way home, but if you'd rather I didn't — well . . . '

'No, it's really kind of you to offer. I don't know about my mother though.'

'Well I wasn't thinking of giving your mother a lift too.' She watched his face for a smile. No, that one didn't quite go as planned. His eyes gave a flicker which might have been minimal amusement, but the rest of his face stayed as serious as ever.

'She should be home by the time you

get there, so that would be good, as it happens. Are you sure you wouldn't mind?'

'Of course not. If no one's in, we'll wait in the driveway.'

'I'll ring and confirm it tomorrow.'

'Fine. Well, OK. Goodbye again.' They stared at each other for a few moments longer, then Mike gave a further small twitch of the lips before setting off towards the checkout.

Kirsty watched his jeans-clad bottom to the end of the butter isle. He was certainly in good nick. Trying to remember what on earth else had been on her mental shopping list, she tore her eyes away.

'Oh, and Kirsty . . . ' He'd paused at the end of the isle.

'Yes?'

'Thanks, thanks a lot.'

Well, he'd managed to remember her name without the prefix 'er'. That had to be a result, surely. Smiling to herself, she wondered if she should add a bottle of champagne to her basket.

3

Toby stood on the smallest diving board. It wasn't even a diving board really, just a board that jutted out a bit over the pool. The knowledge didn't prevent his knees from knocking. He felt sick.

'Now crouch down, Toby,' said Kirsty. 'Crouch down. It's just the same as doing a sitting dive. It's exactly the same distance from the water, only you're over it instead of next to it . . . Now then, hands together to give you a smooth entry, head tucked in. Good! Now, when you're ready — go!'

Toby didn't move a muscle. In his crouched position he could hear the strange echoing sound of Kirsty's voice; he could feel the chlorine-tinged, heavy atmosphere of the pool all around him; see the reflection of the lights sparkling in the turquoise water — but it was as though a grey fog had clouded over his brain and he was suddenly powerless to move.

'Go now, Toby! Don't think about it. Keep your head down and tumble in. You'll be fine.'

Tumble in. Tumble in. The words echoed in his brain. *You'll be fine.*

He didn't feel fine. 'I can't. I'm sorry. I can't,' he said in a small voice.

The water below him was the same turquoise blue of the swimming pool it had always been. He knew it was turquoise — so why did it suddenly look grey? Why did it suddenly seem threatening? Threatening and . . . And?

'Toby? Toby, can you hear me?'

He still couldn't move. How was he going to get back? He hated the water, hated the sparkle, the chemical smell of it. He never wanted to come here again. His body started to shake.

'OK,' came Kirsty's calm voice. 'Don't let's worry about the diving then. Just straighten up slowly to standing and look across the pool at the

55

wall on the other side.'

With a great effort of will Toby complied.

'Don't look down any more. Head up. Good. Now turn slowly and face me. Steady and slow.'

Cautiously, Toby obeyed and found himself staring into Kirsty's unwavering blue gaze. All at once he felt better.

'Excellent. Now walk towards me. It's only two steps. Two steps, that's all. You can do that for me, can't you?'

The blue gaze never faltered. Yes, he could do that for her. One foot in front of the other. He managed it. 'Sorry,' he said when he'd stopped shaking.

'Don't be sorry,' said Kirsty, not touching him or making a fuss or anything. 'No problem. You're allowed to change your mind. Now, I think we'll just slip back into the water and warm ourselves up.

'No,' said Toby firmly. 'I don't think so.'

'Oh come on,' said Kirsty, stripping off her sports pants and top. 'I don't go in with all my pupils, you know.'

Since Toby knew full well that she only went into the water with the babies or the special cases and that she was making an exception for him, he gave a half smile.

'That's more like it,' said Kirsty. 'I've got my best tank-ini on too. D'you like it?'

'It's very orange.'

'It is, isn't it?' Kirsty guided him down the steps and before he knew it he was in the water again, and it was very nearly all right.

'We'll just have a race across the pool. Legs like a frog. Breast stroke or doggy paddle with your arms, up to you.'

And suddenly, even though less than three minutes ago he'd felt sure he'd never swim again, he found himself splashing across the pool with Kirsty's very orange tank-ini never more than an arm's length away. Together they did three more widths, and when he discovered it was time for the end of the lesson he'd almost forgotten that strange moment of awfulness.

Almost, but not quite.

'OK,' said Kirsty. 'We'll leave off the diving for now. No rush, hey? Get yourself changed and I'll see you outside. We'll have a hot chocolate together, shall we?'

'Cool,' answered Toby, even though he was aware that earlier he'd been feeling very uncool indeed.

★　★　★

Kirsty stared at her phone.

Should she ring him?

It wasn't unusual for kids to panic occasionally, but somehow it wasn't like Toby. He wasn't the sort to panic — not like that. He thought things through. He was the kind of child who gave things measured consideration and made a decision accordingly. If he hadn't wanted to step out on that board she was quite certain that, knowing she would never force the issue, he would have said so right away. She knew there was a high enough level of trust between them for that. No, something else had triggered the sudden freezing of his small body.

They hadn't spoken of it again. The chocolate had been consumed with as much gusto as ever and they'd chatted easily together on the journey home. Kirsty had pulled into the now-familiar drive and Grandma Sommerton had come out to greet them with words about the improvement in the weather, and would Toby please remember to empty his swimming bag in the utility room. Of Mike there had been no sign, so Kirsty waved a carefree goodbye and said, 'See you next week then,' and that had been that.

She had hoped to maybe have a quiet word with Anne — she'd discovered Grandma's name by now — but instead of tearing in to greet Buddy, who was barking from somewhere within, Toby had hung around in order to say goodbye to Kirsty, so that opportunity hadn't presented itself. Shame. It would have been easy to confide in Anne, who instead of being white-haired and wrinkled and slightly tubby as she had imagined, turned out to be a well preserved, elegant lady in her late fifties, with a smooth platinum bob and a good figure. She was nice, though, for despite a certain reserve in her manner, her eyes held a twinkle, and the smile she gave Toby was full of love. It made Kirsty feel better to think that Toby had an under-standing Grandma.

There was really no need for her to phone Mike. Surely there wasn't.

Only . . .

Only she felt Mike should know. Felt she should mention it, because it had been somehow disturbing watching Toby's boy shoulder blades still and tense, and sensing his sudden fear. Knowing she'd have no peace until she acted, Kirsty took Mike Sommerton's card from her bag and punched the mobile number into her phone.

'Hello, er, Kirsty.'

So her number was on his phone now. She felt a small glow.

Briefly she explained what had happened at the pool. 'He really wanted to do it,' she said. 'He saw another kid do a somersault off the end of the spring board and thought it was pretty cool, so I suggested he try a duck dive first. He's got quite used to duck dives now even though he didn't like them to start with. So he was quite happy about it at first — but once out on the spring board he just sort of, somehow — froze.'

Mike was quiet for a moment, as though assimilating the facts. 'Well, he seems OK now. He's just gone to bed and he'll soon be fast asleep I expect . . . He always sleeps well after your lessons.'

Kirsty suddenly felt a fool for making what appeared to be a quite unnecessary call. 'Oh good. I thought I'd explain just in case he says he doesn't want to do any more swimming lessons.'

He sounded curt, almost dismissive. 'Thank you for letting me know. I'm sure we'll still keep up with the lessons though.'

There was a small silence. It was no good. The picture of Toby's heels, small boy's bony bottom and back topped by his head of dark hair, crouched at the end of the board and all strangely immobile, would not go away.

'That's not *quite* all.'

'Oh?'

'Well, yes, it *is* why I called, but . . .'

'But what?' There was a sudden anxious edge to his voice.

'I don't know . . . He seemed so lonely out there . . . Look, I know it's none of my business, but I do know when a little boy needs a hug.'

This time the silence was much longer. Kirsty shut her eyes.

'And you don't think I do?' His voice was icy.

'Well, if you didn't know what went on today — no, you might not.'

Silence again.

'Don't think I don't appreciate your concern.' For a moment the cold fury

62

in his voice took her by surprise. 'But I can assure you, if ever I feel the need for your advice I'll ask for it. Toby and me . . . Toby and *I*, we manage fine, thank you. And *I'll* decide when to give him a hug.'

'Right,' said Kirsty, swallowing rapidly. 'Message received. I was only trying to help. I'm — I'm very fond of Toby.'

'Strangely enough, so am I.'

'Well. Good night then.'

'Good night.'

She was shaking, she realised, after clicking her phone off. Whether the shaking was from indignation, humiliation or just from the sound of his voice she wasn't sure, but she had to sit down and recover.

A cup of coffee and half an hour later the shaking had worn off, to be replaced by a feeling of annoyance that she'd let Mike's reaction to what had, after all, only been a well-meaning call, rattle her. It wasn't like her to be so easily upset. Usually she'd just shrug her shoulders and get on with life. Nevertheless,

the evening ahead stretched unattrac-
tively empty and long, so she picked up
her phone again in order to ring her
closest friend Jo, and offload some
bottled-up spleen.

Before she could press a button,
however, her mobile buzzed into life.

'Mission hug completed,' said his
voice in her ear. 'Child in bed and
sleeping soundly.'

'Oh,' said Kirsty, suddenly smiling
broadly. 'I'm sorry Mike, I had no
business interfering.'

'You didn't interfere. My fault for
being so touchy. I really do appreciate
the way you care about Toby.'

'Um,' said Kirsty, who could think of
nothing more profound to say.

'Look, I'd like to explain a bit about
Toby. Are you busy this evening? Could
we perhaps meet up at The Queen's
Head for a drink?'

'Um,' said Kirsty again.

'I thought it might be a bit short
notice. Perhaps some other time?'

Kirsty's heart gave a little flip. Did he

sound a little bit disappointed? 'Hang on a minute,' said Kirsty, wondering how quickly she could strip off her oldest tracksuit and squeeze into skinny jeans and a top. 'I didn't say no. How about in half an hour? Oh, but what about Toby?'

'It's all right, my mother's here. Her suggestion, anyway. She told me I was growing grumpier by the minute and I should apologise for being so high-handed with you and take you for a drink.'

'Oh,' said Kirsty, unsure whether she should be annoyed that he'd needed prompting or grateful that Anne had been there to do it. 'Right, then. I'll see you in a bit.'

★　★　★

The pub was busy for a Wednesday. Mike was sitting at a corner table with a pint of beer in front of him. Unobserved, Kirsty watched him for a moment, her own nervousness fast disappearing because he looked absolutely terrified.

As she approached the table, he looked up and smiled. 'Hello, er, Kirsty,' he said.

'Hi, sorry if I'm a bit late. Couldn't decide between the pink or the green.'

Mike swept her a glance that fleetingly took in the skinny jeans, flat pumps, and pink linen top before landing back on her face, which took rather more of his attention. He smiled again.

'Pink is perfect, although I'm sure green would be equally good. Thank you for coming. What would you like to drink?'

'Oh thanks. I'll just have an orange juice.'

'OK.' He was already on his feet and halfway to the bar. Kirsty settled into her seat and watched him procure her drink. He had a good triangular-shaped back narrowing to firm, slim hips. Tonight he was wearing a grey checked shirt and darker grey jeans. She wondered if he worked out and whether he ever wore anything more adventurous than grey or navy. He was one of the few men of her acquaintance who, with that tan and the silver hair, really would look good in pink.

'So?' she asked, once he'd sat down again.

He looked at her questioningly.

'About Toby?'

'Ah, yes, Toby.' Mike looked back at his drink and lined up his beer mat so that his glass was centralised on it. 'Has he ever spoken about his mother?'

Well, that was a direct question she hadn't been expecting. 'No, no he hasn't. He sometimes mentions his grandma or Saskia, who he told me is your 'or pear', but no, he's never mentioned his mother.'

'Well, I expect you've wondered.'

'Not specially,' said Kirsty, mentally crossing her fingers.

'Of course, I suppose a lot of children come from single-parent families, but Toby's case is a bit different . . . His mother died when he was four.'

Poor little boy. Kirsty's heart gave a lurch. 'That must have been tough.'

Mike cleared his throat and pulled his ear. 'It was. It was an accident, you see. It's not as though we had any warning or could prepare ourselves in any way. And well, being only four, naturally Toby was very close to Louise, counted on her for everything really. How does a small child ever cope with such a loss?'

One of his hands was clenched round his beer glass, the other in a fist on the table. Kirsty dearly would have liked to put a hand out to cover his, but something made her hesitate and the moment passed.

'I think he does extraordinarily well,' she said at length. 'Well, the pair of you do. It must be really hard.'

The fist relaxed a little. 'My mother's marvellous, and my sister and our friends. Especially our friends, given the circumstances . . . We haven't lacked support; don't think that. It's just that

I'm so conscious I must do a good job with Toby. He deserves that at least.'

'Yes,' said Kirsty. 'It must feel like a huge responsibility.'

'It is, but he makes it easy most of the time,' he said to his beer glass. 'He's a good kid.'

'Yes,' agreed Kirsty, wishing he would meet her eyes. It was difficult being sympathetic to someone who wouldn't look at you.

As though reading her thoughts, he suddenly glanced up with a brief smile of relief. 'Thank you . . . I always dread that; the saying 'Louise is dead' bit. It's still hard to explain to people.'

Unsure how to proceed, Kirsty took a sip of her orange.

'Anyway, about Toby's lessons,' he went on. 'If you could just keep an eye on him I'd be grateful. Grateful, too, if you could update me if any more incidents happen. Obviously, I should have realised that if you took the trouble to phone me you must have been worried. I'm sorry I didn't recognise that straight away.'

'Well, I'm glad I did. Phone you, I mean. Because now I know a bit more, it'll help me to understand. He's great, though; never makes a fuss about anything.'

'Funnily enough, he says the same about you.'

'That's nice.'

'Thing is. I've always been conscious that the swimming thing could be a bit tricky. His mother died on holiday, on a beach.'

Her eyes widened with surprise. For some reason she'd imagined a car accident. 'What happened?'

A shadow passed across Mike's face. 'No one knows exactly. There were six of us there. Well, six adults, four children. Tracey and Tim with their three, off down the beach out of sight. On the beach, Nina and Jack, Louise, Toby and me. I was giving it some zeds. What happened? I don't know. I'd been working really hard and I was just zonked out ... The last thing I remember was Louise, in the background, saying she'd take Toby up on the cliffs for a walk. I watched her walk away. Then I fell asleep. Eventually, when she still wasn't back, Nina went to look for them while Jack was swimming. After searching round for a while, during which time it had started to rain, Nina found Toby wandering by himself, crying.'

Totally still, Kirsty sat listening to Mike, who was speaking in a flat voice as if repeating a monologue he had learned by heart.

'I knew something was wrong then,' he went on in the same flat voice. 'Terribly wrong. Louise would never have left Toby to fend for himself if she could possibly help it . . . We called the coast guard. We searched and eventually, hours later, she was found. Somehow she'd fallen, fallen down the cliffs and there she was, splayed out at the bottom — like a broken doll.'

Mike's face was so bleak that this time Kirsty didn't even think about it before she put out a hand and covered his. 'I'm so sorry, Mike. So sorry.'

Mike shot her a quick glance, before sliding his hand from under hers. 'Yeah, well. That's what happened . . . No wonder Toby occasionally has a bleep. I do too.'

'Did he ever see someone afterwards?'

'What d'you mean?'

'Well, he was obviously traumatised . . . I don't know. A counsellor, or something?'

'Yes, I think he did. Sorry, things are still a bit fuzzy about that time . . . Yes, a child psychologist had a few easy words with him at home. And then again later. He's blocked the memory out. The general opinion seemed to be that Toby was a strong little boy and would cope as well as could be expected . . . And we have. It's surprising what you can do if you have to.'

'Yes,' said Kirsty, because there seemed nothing else to say.

'Only, he never mentions Louise much anymore . . . They told me that would happen. Children are very resilient; they soon accept things as they are. Probably when he's older he'll want to know more. But for now, she's just a sad but pleasant, warm memory to him.'

'So, he completely went off swimming, and water I suppose, for a while?'

'Funny enough, no, not really. He was happy to go to the beach again, although we've never been back to exactly the place it happened. That's a no-no. But he's not as adventurous as he used to be, certainly, which is why I wanted him to have the lessons to give him confidence and bring him up to speed.' He gave a small smile. 'I have to be honest with you. He wasn't at all keen to have the private lessons. He said they were only for babies.'

'Most of my pupils think that until I teach them different.'

Mike took a drink from his beer glass, replacing it carefully on its mat.

'The same crowd of us still go there every year. My great aunt had a place there that she left to Mum, Sam and me near Ilfracombe in Devon. We've been going every year for ten years or more. Rightly or wrongly, I decided not to change things, so we continue to go. Toby plays with Tracey and Tim's children as usual. Sometimes my mum comes with us or my sister . . . And Saskia comes with us, then goes back to Poland for her own holiday while I take time off with Toby. It's nice to have another adult around in order to keep the numbers even. Somehow it helps.' He took another swift gulp from his glass and attempted a grin. 'But enough about me and Toby. Tell me about you.'

Kirsty wrinkled her nose. 'That might be a bit boring, but what would you like to know?'

'Anything. I hardly know a thing other than that you tell jokes that make Toby laugh and he never knows what colour hair you'll turn up with.'

'Very good. There's not much else to

tell. I love my job. Of course I do. Wish it paid a bit more, but then I remember working in a call centre once and hating every moment of it, so . . . '

'What made you decide to teach swimming?'

'Oh, it's not just swimming. My talents are many and wide-ranging. I do varied group exercise classes. Pilates, water aerobics, stretch and tone workouts, oh lots of different things, and if you want a personal trainer — I'm your girl. Not that you look as though you need it. You seem in pretty good shape to me.' *Careful, Kirsty*, she told herself. *You're practically flirting with him.*

He ignored the flirting, if that was what it was. 'Well, if you're lucky enough to find a job that suits you, I'd say stick to it.'

'Yeah well, I didn't have a deal of choice, but I managed to get my qualifications, so as long as I keep my books straight — which, with a bit of help from my so-clever brother, I do — I'm pretty much my own boss.'

'I'd agree there. I work for myself too.'

'Ah yes, you make kitchens.'

'I do. Good kitchens, as it happens. I thought that with the recession, my workload would go down, but because I work at the top end of the market it seems I'm OK. Rather than move house, those who can afford it are extending their kitchens or going for completely new ones, which is great. Nothing I like more than designing and making a good quality kitchen.'

'Hm,' said Kirsty, thinking of her at least ten-year-old kitchen by the look of it, that she fully intended to paint lime-green just as soon as she had the time. 'I suppose you need to know about geometry and things for that? Definitely maths?'

'Technical drawing, computer skills and common sense are more useful actually.'

'Sounds terrible. I slogged away for years at my family's insistence to try and make the grade in maths. Never did manage it though.'

'Who cares, so long as you're happy, and you obviously are.' He looked at her for a long moment. 'You always look so carefree. Life's easy to you, isn't it?'

Why did people always think that because she didn't go around being miserable all the time, her life was a bunch of roses? Nevertheless, Kirsty smiled. 'Not especially, no. I'm a bit dyslexic. A bit slow on the uptake. Memory appalling. It caused me a lot of grief through my school years.' Briefly, as she recalled the struggles she'd had with spelling tests and mental arithmetic, her eyes shadowed. 'But hey.' Her face brightened. 'Then I discovered I could run and do well at most sports. My parents sent me to a sports college. They feel guilty, you see. They're both clever, and my brother's bright. They tried their best with me but I could see them wondering, where on earth had I come from?'

'But they must be pleased for you now.'

'Think so.' She wrinkled her nose

again. 'But my mother doesn't really think it's a proper job. She keeps asking what I'll do when I get too old to carry on at the rate I do.'

Mike laughed, his grey-green eyes creasing at the corners. 'Well you don't have to worry about keeping up the pace for a good while. How old are you, anyway?'

'Thirty-one.'

An expression of pure astonishment passed over his face. 'Really? I thought you were about twenty-four.'

'Thanks for that. And?'

'And what?'

'Well, the least you can do is to return the compliment.'

Mike laughed again and, looking vaguely embarrassed, tugged at his ear. 'Oh well, all right then. I'm thirty-six.'

'Really?'

'Oh, I know . . . It's the grey hair, isn't it?'

'Well, at first I did have you down as older. Pushing forty, I thought. But now I've got to know you a bit more and realise you don't look angry all the time, so I'd have said about thirty-six-ish.'

Mike passed a hand over his thick short-cropped hair. 'It's in the genes, I'm afraid. My mother went grey at thirty but she's had the help of the hairdresser ever since.'

'Your mother has the most beautiful skin,' said Kirsty. 'You've inherited that from her too, so it's not all bad. Anyway it's a nice dark grey with silver high-lights. Distinguished-looking.'

She liked the way his mouth curled upwards when he was slightly embarrassed. It made him look more approachable, almost boyish. 'You've made me feel better now,' he said with another grin. 'I did consider dying it once, after one of Toby's school friends thought I was his granddad.' He laughed a little sheepishly. 'Only, somehow it felt a bit seedy to think about dying my hair. Anyway, what d'you mean? I do not always look angry!'

'All right then, *nearly* always,' said

Kirsty with a grin.

And suddenly it was easy, sitting here with Mike listening to him talking about setting up his business. How he'd had to work sometimes twelve hours a day in order to make it profitable, how he'd had to search for premises to house some kind of showroom with a workplace behind. He loved to work with wood, he said — oak being his favourite, but beech and ash also being good. The new laminates coming in were not so much up his street, but he was learning to like them because a lot of his most trendy clients did, and you had to move with the times.

He was a good listener, too. Suddenly Kirsty found herself telling him that the pink in her hair was what she thought of as her rebellious streak. 'I can wash it out if I want,' she explained. 'I considered a ring through my nose once, just to annoy my brother, really — he's very disapproving — but then I thought about the pain, and who was I hurting, really? Anyway, I'm past all that now. I quite like the hair dye still, but I just like bright colours and wear them because they make people smile.'

They chatted on. He asked her if she'd like another drink and, because her throat had got dry from talking — and besides, she'd discovered that she was enjoying herself too much to want to go home quite yet — she said yes, she would.

Eventually though, after they'd had another drink each and realised that the clientele were thinning, Mike glanced at his watch with surprise. 'Is that really the time? I must go.' He pushed his chair back.

'OK, Cinderella,' said Kirsty. 'I understand you have to be back on the stroke of — let's see — eleven thirty.'

'Sorry,' said Mike, immediately contrite. 'That was so rude. I've had a lovely evening. The time went so quickly that I was surprised, that's all.'

'So have I — had a lovely evening,' said Kirsty, picking up her orange bag. 'Lovely.'

His grey-green eyes stared into hers for a moment longer. 'It might be nice to do it again sometime.'

'Yes,' said Kirsty, her heart beating wildly. 'It might be very nice.'

4

He'd said they should do it again sometime. Of course, he hadn't really meant
it, Kirsty told herself repeatedly over the
next few days. He was just being polite,
that was all. *Let's face it, Kirsty, Mike is
still a grieving widower. The last thing
he is thinking of is romance.*

But it had been four years, hadn't it?
Time to move on, surely? Anyway, they
had nothing in common — only Toby.
And he was so serious. What did she
want with serious, anyway? Hadn't
she always been a fun person? Always
up for a laugh? Mike hardly looked as
though he knew how to laugh.

Then, remembering his sudden grin,
the corner of his eyes wrinkling with
amusement, she admitted that he probably did have a sense of humour hidden
away somewhere. Perhaps he was just
out of practice. This made her think of

other things he might be out of practice at and she found her face burning and her heart performed a few sudden cartwheels — but still her phone remained silent.

The next swimming lesson came and went. Although a little nervous, Toby tried particularly hard to please her but they both kept well away from all talk of duck dives or diving boards.

'Of course, Mike was only being polite,' said Kirsty to Jo, her pretty dark haired-friend when they met for a drink two days after the swimming lesson. 'I know that.'

'But you hoped that wasn't all he was being, didn't you?' replied Jo with a knowing glance. 'There once was a man so polite

He never got anything right
He passed up the chance
To ask a girl for a dance
And ended up having a fight.'

'Very funny, and fast too,' said Kirsty. 'But, he is kind of nice. The sort who

grows on you. Doesn't smile very much
— that was a bit of a worry — but now
I understand why. And when he does
smile, he's pretty attractive.'

'Make your mind up. Is he pretty or
attractive?'

'Anyway,' went on Kirsty, completely
ignoring her, 'it's not his looks. It's just
him. In spite of the forbidding outside,
there's something about him I somehow take to, and Toby's just so
sweet . . . '

'Careful,' said Jo. 'Don't let your
feelings for Toby get mixed up with
your feelings for Mike.'

Kirsty flushed. 'Of course not,' she said.
'I'm much too professional for that. What
I meant was, it's not as though there's
some child in the mix that's an unknown
quantity. I already know Toby. I know
the situation. Toby already likes me.'

'But let's not forget — he hasn't
called you in what, over a week?'

'No, I know. But he didn't say he
would.'

For a long moment Jo contemplated

her drink. 'So, let's recap. You phoned him because you were worried about his son. He choked you off on the phone, then later rang back and took you out for a drink in order to apologise. And you went — just like that. Dropped everything, right?'

'Yes, but . . . '

'I'm just telling it like it is. You had the drink. He told you the history; you had a chat about this and that. End of story. Or was it?' Her dark eyes opened wider. 'Did he kiss you good night?'

A blush tided over Kirsty's face. 'No, of course not. He just said it would be nice to do it again. The drink bit, I mean.'

'But as you said he was just being polite. You're blushing, by the way.'

Kirsty pulled a face. 'Well, if you put it like that, I suppose I was reading too much into it, and I am not blushing. It's hot in here, that's all.'

'Yeah, yeah . . . ' Jo gave her a long, thoughtful glance. 'He's been, what — four years without a wife? And you drop into his lap, looking gorgeous. You obviously like his son and his son likes you — bonus points, I'd say. I'd have thought if he were interested, he'd be back on that phone so fast you wouldn't have even had time to draw breath.'

To cover the sinking of her heart telling her that every word she was hearing was true, Kirsty took a swallow of wine. Trust Jo to be right. She always was. 'OK. He probably doesn't fancy me. He probably just regards me as Toby's swimming teacher, who's nice enough to pass the time of day with. The only way he'll ever think of me is as a good mate ... Story of my life really, isn't it? Anyway, thanks for the looking gorgeous bit, I needed that.'

'Well, you are gorgeous and I wish you'd let me fix you up with one of Paul's mates. They're all champing at the bit to meet you again. Especially Ed.'

'We've had this conversation before, and the answer is 'no'. Match-making between friends doesn't work. It makes it so awkward for everyone when we find out — which we always do — that we don't like each other that much.'

Jo gave a pretend pout. 'It's not like you to be so negative.'

'I know, but listen. You've found Paul and I'm really happy for you, but I don't need a man in my life. I'm completely happy without one. All right I'll admit it, I'm attracted to this guy Mike, but that doesn't mean I'll die of a broken heart if he's not interested. I can accept that he's unsuitable, unavailable and uninterested . . . '

'*Dis*interested,' corrected Jo, who was a teacher. '*U*ninteresting, but *dis*interested.'

'Yes, that . . . And even though he's undeniably attractive, I don't have to start desperately searching online for a boyfriend, just because he didn't call me . . . '

Her friend of more years than either of them cared to remember, contemplated her from over the rim of her wineglass. 'Course not,' she said. 'I know that. I just wonder whether you're getting a bit too involved — emotionally, I mean. I thought one of Paul's mates might take your mind off this Heathcliff character and you'd get back into the real world.'

Kirsty didn't answer, because the truth was she'd really expected Mike to be in touch by now. She'd thought he'd enjoyed the evening as much as she had. She'd allowed herself to imagine that he'd want to see her again pretty quickly; that he might have kept thinking about her, even when his mind should be on something else. That, like her, he'd catch himself humming a tune that had been playing in the pub, remembering certain snatches of conversation, certain changes of expression, and the occasional meeting of glances that said, 'I like you, I really do.'

Get a grip, she told herself. 'My glass seems to be empty,' she said to Jo. 'I'll get another round and you can tell me about how it went with Paul's parents.'

'We're going to have a barbecue,' said Toby.

'That's nice,' Kirsty answered mechanically.

'And we're going to build a pond.'

'Lovely.'

'It's because it's Whitsun and we're both having a holiday and Grandma will still be here to help, and Sam's coming — she's always fun.'

'Sam?' asked Kirsty, her ears pricking up. She might have known it. Mike already had a girlfriend; and after all, why shouldn't he have?

'My dad's sister. I think she's my auntie, but I always call her Sam.'

Kirsty felt a stirring of relief. She remembered now — Sam was the fun auntie. 'Well, when you're ready, Toby, we'll try that width again. And this time I want you to concentrate on your breathing. In as you pull back, and out as you glide forward. Good. Now *pull* those arms back. Excellent! Your arms are getting

90

much stronger — good work!'

So, Mike wasn't going to call her. He had, after all, just been being polite.

She carried on with the swimming lesson. Once again, no mention was made about diving, 'duck' or otherwise. Kirsty wasn't sure quite what she'd been expecting, but the freezing episode of two weeks ago didn't seem to be bothering Toby in the least now. As far as he was concerned, it might never have happened.

When the lesson ended, they had their hot chocolate — or rather Toby did, as Kirsty contented herself with a glass of water — and then made their way to the car. She didn't feel like telling jokes on the way home, so instead she recited 'The Owl and the Pussy Cat', which she'd learned by heart as a child and managed all the way through to the end in spite of Toby's interruption of, 'What's 'runcible' mean?'

'A runcible spoon is really a three-pronged fork with a rounded edge,' explained Kirsty, pulling into the paved driveway.

'Oh,' said Toby. 'Probably invented

for barbecues, so you can prong your sausages and scoop up your beans at the same time ... Did I ask?' Toby broke off. 'Oh, Dad's home!'

Kirsty's foot slipped a bit on the brake. 'Oh yes,' she said, moistening her lips and wishing she'd paid a little more attention to her hair. Quick as a flash, Toby was out of the car and had attached himself to Mike at waist level. Smiling rather more widely than usual, Mike ruffled his son's hair, all the time looking at Kirsty.

Should she get out? Would it look too obvious? Deciding that it would, Kirsty wound down the window instead. She left the engine running so as not to appear too eager.

'Hi, Mike.'

'Hi there!'

So that was to be it? Nothing more, then? Not 'how are you' or 'I've missed you'? *She wished!*

'Well?' Mike turned his attention to Toby.

'I did all right, didn't I?' said Toby,

looking at Kirsty.

'Sure did, kiddo,' said Kirsty, wondering just when she had turned into an American. 'Very all right.'

'Well, did you ask her?' Mike was still looking at Toby.

Apparently mystified, Toby looked back.

'To the barbecue, dumb nut,' said Mike, cuffing Toby gently on his shoulder.

'Oh no,' said Toby. 'I started to, but then I forgot.'

'Oh right,' said Mike, manoeuvring Toby by his shoulders into a shield-like position in front of him. 'He was going to ask you to come to our place on Saturday. We're having a few family and friends round for a barbie.' He pulled at his ear. 'But I told Toby he mustn't count on it — you might be busy.'

Kirsty licked her lips again. 'No, I'm not busy. Not at all. I'd love to come.'

'You can bring someone,' said Toby.

'But you don't have to,' added Mike rather swiftly. 'On your own would be good.'

Kirsty's heart started pounding. For a moment she'd thought he was going to say, 'On your own would be better.'

She gave a wide grin. 'On my own it is, then. What time?'

'In the afternoon. Three-ish, we thought.'

'I'll look forward to it,' said Kirsty.

★ ★ ★

'Ha!' said Kirsty as soon as Jo answered.

'Ha, as in, funny ha-ha?'

'Ha, as in, I was right! Mike's just asked me to a family barbecue!'

'Great,' said Jo. 'What are you going to wear?'

'That's what I love about you. You're so shallow.'

'Come to think of it, as it's a barbecue you don't need my advice; all your clothes are barbecue clothes.'

'Yep!' said Kirsty happily. 'Anyway, he doesn't mind about the clothes. He likes bright.'

'Did he actually say that, or did he just — not say he didn't like bright?'

'I thought, actually, red shorts or skinny jeans and a nice gaudy top to liven it up.'

'Not orange though, please. Not orange with red! Take some beer and some flowers for his mum. Always a nice touch. Mums love flowers.'

'Thanks for that. I'll ring later if I need any more advice.' Kirsty clicked off and, much to Tiger's amazement, picked him up and danced across the kitchen. 'He does like me, Tiger, he does, he does!'

* * *

Toby sat in the corner, playing with Sam's iPad. Buddy was watching him with his head on one side.

'So what's she like, then?' said Sam to Toby's grandma, who was busy counting plates and paper serviettes.

'Who?'

'Kirsty. D'you know, I've always liked the name Kirsty. Why didn't you call me Kirsty? Kirsty Sommerton sounds more theatrical than Sam Sommerton.'

'You can always change it,' said Grandma.

'Bit late now. Anyway, I've got a billing part in a small revue.'

'How small?'

'Very,' said Sam with a laugh. 'Anyway, what's she like?'

'Blonde, lovely smile, very good figure.'

'Goodness. Really?'

'More to the point, she's nice. I like her.'

'OK, well that's good. Hey Tobes, what you doing there?'

'Turning all the photos funny. Look, you can make them red and green — or like this, blue and pink.'

'How d'you do that? I think this child's a genius. I've had this iPad a month; he's only just set eyes on it. Show me how you did that, Tobes.'

'It's easy,' said Toby with a small sense of pride. He liked Sam. She often told him he was a genius, but in a nice way, not a making fun way — just as though she was on the verge of actually believing it. Of course Toby knew he wasn't a genius, but sometimes he did feel as though he could be pretty clever. He'd like to be cool as well as clever, but recognised that as long as there were other kids in his class who already had iPads of their own — not to mention mobiles with all the latest technology, and the right football boots, and hair that their mothers gelled every morning — he didn't really have much hope of that.

The doorbell rang. Toby hoped it might be Tim and Tracey with Jenny, Brad and Rosie — although Jenny had suddenly become quite grown up, and was always on about the latest song, and had a thing about bags. He couldn't think why. What did a twelve-year-old girl put in a bag with a leopard-skin front and a chain handle, for goodness sake? Brad, though, was still the same Brad; and even though he was nine, he treated eight-year-old Toby as though he was an equal. Brad thought everything was awesome and could travel on a skateboard with some serious pace. And Rosie . . . Well, she was just Rosie. If Toby had had a sister he would have quite liked her to be Rosie.

But as soon as the door had been answered, he could tell it wasn't them. It was Nina. The only good thing about Nina was that she had a really cool red sports car. He wished his dad had one like it. Nina herself, however, was a different matter. Toby heard her voice rising to an excited squeak as she said hello to everyone. He could imagine her kissing the air at each side of every person she passed as she made her way through to the back of the house. Looking for an escape route and finding none, Toby shrank further into his corner. He stared fixedly at the iPad screen.

'Ah, my favourite man-child,' said Nina in a high voice as though she was speaking to a baby. 'Hello, Tobes.'

''Lo,' said Toby out of the side of his mouth, praying that she wouldn't kiss him. He knew Grandma would be giving him that look which meant that he should get up and be polite because Nina was a guest. But because he somehow also knew that Grandma had a certain pinched expression on her face whenever Nina was around, he only very slowly got to his feet, put the iPad on the counter, and then managed to slide away, muttering something about helping Dad with the barbecue.

'Hi, Tobes!' Dad stood at the barbecue, looking at the smoking coals. He was looking cheerful today in a white shirt and khaki shorts. 'Brad not here yet, then?'

'No,' said Toby. 'Neither is Kirsty. Sam thinks Kirsty is a nice name.'

'Well, she's a nice person,' said Dad. 'She deserves a nice name.'

'Who does?'

Toby's heart sank. He might have guessed it wouldn't take long for Nina to catch up with them. Watching as she positioned herself unnecessarily close and kissed his father's cheek, Toby cringed. 'Anyone I should know?' She was talking in her little girl playful voice again, the one that Toby hated. Why did she talk like that to him and his dad?

'My swimming teacher,' he said coldly, fixing her with a look. 'I asked her to come because I like her; she tells good jokes.'

'I'm sure she does,' said Nina. 'Does she teach you to swim, too?'

What sort of stupid question was that? Toby looked away without answering. Then his face lit up. 'Here's Brad,' he said with relief.

*   *   *

There was no doubt about it, Kirsty was nervous. She'd tried on some white shorts she knew she looked good in and teamed them with a black sleeveless shirt. These were the most subdued summer clothes she possessed, but somehow she just didn't feel right. She took the black shirt off and replaced it with a scoop-necked purple top — sort of sporty, but silky. A little more feminine, perhaps? She looked in the mirror and smiled. That felt so much better. She'd scraped her hair into its usual ponytail, because she wasn't sure about loose hair and shorts. That the pink streak picked up the pink of the large flower stencilled on the front of her top was a happy accident, but she still looked a bit fitness instructor-ish. On a whim she pinned a white artificial flower behind her ear.

It had just gone three and she was almost ready to go. Now, the pink bag or the white? Or what about the orange? Oh darn it. Yeah — the orange! Trying not to imagine Jo's wince of disapproval, Kirsty put the beers in her bag and picked up the flowers she'd bought earlier.

There were several cars, including a nifty, sporty red Lotus parked on one side of the drive, and she could smell the barbecue as soon as she got out of her car. So that was all right, then; she hadn't got the wrong day. But just outside the wrought iron side-gate which led, by the looks of it, to the side garden, she had a small crisis of confidence as to whether to go through or ring the front doorbell.

'Oh come in this way,' said a tall, sandy-haired man through the bars of the gate. He was holding the hand of a small girl of about six or seven, who smiled shyly at her. 'My name's Tim, and this is Rosie. Can I make a guess that you're Toby's swimming teacher?'

Kirsty bent down. 'Hello, Rosie — that's a very pretty dress you're wearing. I like the glittery bits . . . You're right,' she went on to Tim. 'How did you know?' She straightened up and grinned with relief that she'd been accepted so easily by this by this smiling, friendly man.

'Easy. Toby told me you were pretty and probably had pink hair.'

'Take no notice of Tim; he's a renowned flirt,' said Mike, coming towards them with a fork in one hand and a beer in the other. 'I suppose I'll have to trust him to get you a drink, because I'm all caught up with the barbecue.'

At the sight of him, his shorts and T-shirt showing his physique to its full advantage, Kirsty felt her heart give a lurch. 'Fine,' she said. 'Smells good.' She tore her eyes away from him in case they gave away how much she'd wanted to see him again; how she'd longed for exactly this warm feeling that was making its way up her spine. 'Um, I need to just find your mother. I've brought her some flowers.'

'She'll like that,' said Mike, the George Clooney lines at the sides of his cheeks making a sudden appearance. 'I'll catch up with you in just a bit, promise. Tim will make the introductions.'

'Love to,' said Tim who for some reason of his own was staring at Mike and grinning like the Cheshire Cat. 'First I'll find Anne, then I'll introduce you to my wife Tracey — she's that beautiful redhead over there.'

Kirsty looked across in the direction

Tim indicated and saw a tall, friendly-looking lady engaged in conversation with a sultry brunette. Crikey, even Jo would be gobsmacked by the sultry brunette's outfit. Top-notch designer, caramel-coloured linen. The sort of dress you needed make-up and attitude to carry off. The glossy brunette had plenty of both.

Kirsty blinked and tore her eyes away. Tracey had looked up at the mention of her name and was coming towards her now with her hand out stretched. It proved to be as easy to warm to Tracey as to her husband. Kirsty smiled and agreed that the weather looked set to stay fair; and then, aware of the scrutiny being lavished on her by the brunette, she turned to say hello.

'This is Nina.'

'Hello, Nina.'

Nina had an amused expression in her eyes and Kirsty would have put money on her having summed up the financial value of every item of clothing on Kirsty's back. *Touché*, thought Kirsty.

'Ah, the swimming teacher.'

'That's right,' agreed Kirsty, wondering if she should have worn a label in order to stop Mike's guests asking.

'Tobes has told me all about you,' went on Nina, flicking back her immaculate hair with an equally immaculate, blood-red fingernail. 'Tobes and I are very close, you know.'

'That's nice,' Kirsty said, thinking that actually she didn't really think it was nice — there was something a little scary about Nina. 'I must find Anne,' she said. 'These flowers need some water.'

Nina cast them a cursory glance. 'Mmm, buy them from a garage, did you?'

What a cheek! Seething inside, Kirsty smiled to show she wasn't offended. 'No, a supermarket actually. I so loved the colours, I couldn't resist them.'

'Yes, I can see you love colour,' said Nina, staring pointedly at the orange bag slung casually across the shoulder of Kirsty's purple top.

But these were Mike's friends; she

refused to be offended. 'You'd make a good detective,' she said laughingly.

A dark hedgehogy head arrived at her shoulder. 'Oh great! You came.' Grinning all over his face, Toby pulled at her arm. 'Come and see Brad. He's awesome on a skateboard. Dad said we can have a go on the drive as long as we keep away from the cars. Have you ever been on a skateboard?'

With relief, Kirsty turned her attention to him. 'Well, only my brother's, but I daresay I'll remember. I must just take these flowers to your grandma first.'

'I know where she is; follow me,' said Toby importantly.

With a small wave to Mike, who she could see was half-watching her from the barbecue, Kirsty followed Toby, who was finding his way through the other guests to the large expanse of glass doors that were at the back of the house. But all the time she was uncomfortably aware that Nina's cat-like eyes were looking from Mike to her and back again.

'Oh, here you are; I'm so glad you came.' With a warm smile, Anne took the flowers from her and found a tall vase in the utility room in order to display them. 'There, they're really lovely. Such gorgeous colours. I'll put them on the windowsill. Now Toby, take Kirsty back outside and make sure she meets Sam. I'm sure they'll get on really well.'

Kirsty followed Toby outside and soon found herself swallowed up amongst more guests. She spotted Nina across the other side of the patio and surreptitiously watched as she made her way from group to group, smilingly bestowing her favours on this one and that. Occasionally she laughed and threw her head back in a way that showed off her neck and throat to their best advantage. Most of Mike's guests appeared to be eating out of her hand. Her charm appeared to be effortless; but, Kirsty thought, although it was laid on so thickly that you could cut it with a knife, in reality it was veneer-thin. Resolutely, she looked away and concentrated on the rest of Mike's friends, whom she found she preferred the look of. Generally, she found liking people easy. She particularly took to fun Aunt Sam who, despite being slightly theatrical in manner, had a natural sense of humour and was straightforward and kind to all the children present. Kirsty, who had the same instinctive affinity with children, warmed to her immediately.

Once they'd all been fed with burgers and sausages, Tim took over the barbecue for any second helpings, and Mike brought his plate of food over to where Kirsty was sitting with Anne and his sister Sam.

'Lovely sausages,' said Sam. 'I simply must have another one, although I shouldn't really; I'm getting far too fat.' Since this was patently untrue, Kirsty lifted her eyes to the sky and said that she wished she was that kind of fat.

'Take no notice of my crazy sister.

She's as mad as a box of frogs, always thinking she'll diet. She never does, though, because she knows she doesn't need to. It's just her way of fishing for compliments.'

'Beast,' said Sam, complacently spearing a sausage off Mike's plate and tucking into it. 'No Jack today then?' she went on, as her eyes strayed to where Nina was sitting talking to Tracey and Tim.

'No,' answered Mike shortly. 'I think he's in the States working.'

'He's always working. I haven't seen him for ages.' Sam wrinkled her nose. 'Well, seems like ages. Mind you, I don't blame him. Nina's getting more poisonous by the minute.'

'Sam!' said Anne and Mike in unison.

'Well, you can't fail to notice. She's just so wrapped up in herself all the time. So self-obsessed . . . And that 'I love you all' act, well . . . '

'I think that'll do for now,' said Anne quietly. 'We have a guest.'

'All right, Mum. I spoke out of turn. I wouldn't like Kirsty to be put off by thinking we have many friends like Nina, that's all.' She looked across at her brother, who was grimly staring into his glass. 'Sorry, Mike. I know she was Louise's best friend, but she gives me the ache.'

Oh dear. Kirsty looked at Sam with renewed warmth, glad that she wasn't the only one not to fall for Nina's special form of charm, but there was still an awkward pause. Then Mike looked up with a sudden smile. 'I'll show you the garden, Kirsty, shall I?'

'Sure, I'd like that.' Barely stopping to pick up her drink, Kirsty followed Mike away from the patio, across the lawn towards a deep flower bed. 'Lovely,' she said, although it really wasn't all that special.

'You're very polite, but it's not going to stay like this. This is where the pond's going to go.'

'Oh, a pond?'

'Yes. Not a massive one. But I've been promising Toby a pond for ages now, so being as it's Whitsun this week, we're going to mark it out and make a start. It needs to be in the sun and away from the trees, you see. It'll get lots of blanket weed at first, but once the lily pads give it some shade, it'll be good.'

'Should be fun,' said Kirsty.

'You sounded almost as though you meant that.'

'I did mean it.'

For a long moment their eyes met. There was a questioning expression in his and a quietly encouraging one in hers.

'Would you . . . I mean, would you like to help?'

Kirsty took a deep breath, but Mike pulled at his ear and turned away with an embarrassed laugh. 'I can't believe I actually said that.'

'Well, I'd like to,' said Kirsty softly. 'Help, I mean. If Toby doesn't mind.'

He looked back as though scarcely able to believe his luck. 'Would you really? I mean, I don't expect you to dig all day — of course not. I thought it would be good to hire a small digger.

I've already made a plan.'

She laughed. 'I guessed you would have done, being a kitchen designer and all. Is it going to be modern? I mean, formal I think they call it — straight lines, slabbed edge, or what?'

'Wildlife, I thought,' said Mike, all at once looking quite boyish in his enthusiasm. 'Toby would like that. He'd like watching the tadpoles, the newts and diving beetles, and things. So, I suppose curved edges — kidney-shaped.' He paced out a ten-foot span. 'Only about this width, maybe. By twelve or so feet long.'

'Needs to be bigger. Everyone who makes a pond wishes they'd made it bigger.'

'Really?'

Their eyes met again and a fluttering feeling started in Kirsty's stomach.

'Is this a private conversation, or can anyone join in?' It was Nina again. Silently, Kirsty ground her teeth.

'No,' said Mike. 'It's not private. I was telling Kirsty about the pond Toby and I are going to make.'

'Riveting,' said Nina with a shrug of her elegant shoulder. 'Meanwhile, I think your guests are ready for more burgers. You can't leave poor old Tim holding the fort for ever, you know.' She gave a tinkling laugh and patted his arm.

Before Kirsty could open her mouth to ask why not, as Tim seemed to be making a good job of it, Mike said, 'I suppose not. Oh well . . . Duty calls. I'll catch you later, Kirsty.'

Wondering if it looked as false as the one Nina was also wearing, Kirsty kept her smile on her lips as she watched him go. As Nina stepped closer, a waft of expensive perfume mixed in with the smoky aroma of the barbecue to strange effect. Kirsty cringed a little. Nina turned to face her, the red gash of her lips stretched into what, from a distance, could pass for a friendly smile.

She leaned closer. 'Mike's a very good friend of mine, Chrissie, or Candy, or whatever your name is. Very good, if you take my meaning . . . So any ideas you might have had about cosying up to him, forget them, right?' Nina paused and scrutinised Kirsty from head to toe. Then she leaned forward, for all the world as though she were about to pay her a delightful compliment. 'You're a pretty girl, Candy, but get this — he's way out of your league!'

Shock tided over Kirsty. Then, because she knew she couldn't let the poisonous Nina get away with such bullying tactics, she smiled as sweetly as she could. 'I knew a girl who went to your charm school, Nina,' she said quietly. 'She could lay the charm on, thick and honeyed.'

With a puzzled look in her eyes, Nina took a step back.

'She came to a sticky end!' Kirsty smiled a bright smile.

Nina stared at her, looking completely baffled.

'Only a joke. You know, *honey*, *sticky*? Oh, where's your sense of humour?' Registering the expression of annoyance on Nina's face, Kirsty laughed and walked away.

Good, she'd hit the spot.

5

Nina had gone. Mingling with the other guests and paying spasmodic but not wholly welcomed attention to Toby, Kirsty noticed that Nina had hung around for nearly another hour after issuing the warning off — immediately after which, Kirsty had considered making an excuse and leaving the party early. Then her obstinate streak made itself felt and she'd fixed a bright smile on her face and busied herself helping Anne in the kitchen. But although she'd deliberately avoided looking in Nina's direction, Kirsty had found herself aware of her presence in a way that felt, if not exactly threatening, then certainly unnerving.

But it was nice to see Toby behaving like any other eight-year-old boy. He had a half-eaten burger in one hand and racing around with Brad and teasing Jenny, who was twelve going on fifteen at the beginning of the barbecue — but a couple of hours later had turned back into a kid and was showing off on her brother's skate board, not caring too much where the precious, ultimate-in-cool bag had got to.

With the exception of Nina, they were a nice crowd, Kirsty thought. The kind of crowd her friend Jo would like. Ordinary people who seemed to enjoy life and got on with things in a way that even her own family, who could be picky about her friends, would approve of. But more than that, they had made Kirsty feel welcome, and included her in their conversation as though she were indeed a friend of long-standing.

She'd watched Nina give a cursory goodbye wave to the crowd, lean over Mike to kiss his cheek, and attempt to do the same to Toby, who'd flinched and moved fractionally away. Briefly, over the top of Toby's dark head, Nina's feline eyes met Kirsty's.

Kirsty felt a cold shiver go through

her. There was something in the look that made her realise she'd made a powerful enemy.

Don't be ridiculous, she told herself. *What on earth can she do to you?*

Nevertheless, sitting here now with a throw over her shoulders — although the evening was fine, the air had turned chill — she was glad that Nina had gone. Glad that Nina wasn't here to see that it was Mike who'd fetched the throw and draped it round her shoulders, and Mike who was sitting next to her now, laughing with her over some sort of nonsense that Sam was entertaining them all with.

The barbecue had died down, but Mike had lit the outside wood burner which was burning brightly, setting off sparks now and then and crackling and popping enough to make you jump. Covertly studying his side view, as with a sigh he leaned back in his garden chair, Kirsty thought she had never seen Mike appear so relaxed. Sipping at his beer from time to time, he smiled lazily round at his remaining guests.

Tracey and Tim were sitting next to him in a circle, along with a couple of neighbours whose names Kirsty had forgotten, and Anne and Sam. The children and Buddy were in an untidy heap at the television-end of the large open-plan kitchen, an occasional shout of laughter traveling from them to the outside group.

I really ought to be going, she thought, as she realised that the people left were really those closest to Mike. She looked towards Anne for guidance, but Anne was watching her son with an expression of weary relief in her eyes.

'Um,' said Kirsty. 'I think I should be going.'

'What's the rush?' asked Sam. 'I've hardly got to know you. I'm waiting for one of your famous jokes.'

Kirsty blushed. 'I'm hardly a stand-up comedian,' she said.

'Tobes certainly thinks so.'

'Well, Toby's got a lovely sense of fun but well, you know kids . . . Hardly a good judge.'

'I don't know,' said Sam. 'He doesn't take to people easily and he's certainly taken to you.'

'Yes, well . . . ' Kirsty got to her feet. This conversation was getting uncomfortable, and she was determined not to outstay her welcome. 'It's been lovely. I've enjoyed meeting you all.' She turned towards Anne. 'Thanks so much, Anne, for all your hard work.'

'Well thanks for your help in the kitchen. Nice of you to give me a hand with the glasses.'

'It was a pleasure,' said Kirsty, because it had been. She collected her bag from the kitchen and called goodbye in the general direction of Toby. His face was screwed up in concentration, his eyes fixed on the screen where some game was going on. His reply was his funny little salute, which she guessed would have to do.

There was a chorus of farewells from the circle of chairs outside. Mike was already on his feet. 'I'll see you to your car.'

'It's OK. I can use the side-gate.'

'Well, anyway.' Mike opened the wrought iron gate and followed her out to the front of the house. They could still hear the noise from the party, but that didn't stop the sudden realisation that, for the first time that day, they were alone and out of sight. The tangy, woody smell of the barbecue was still in the air, mixed now with the scent of the rose that wound its way up a trellis beside the gate.

'Thanks so much for coming,' he said.

'Thanks for inviting me,' replied Kirsty, willing herself not to look too obviously at his totally kissable mouth, which had been driving her mad for the last half hour.

'I meant to tell you earlier how nice you look.'

'Um, thank you,' said Kirsty, knowing never to argue over a compliment, just to accept gracefully. 'You do too. Look in pretty good shape, I mean.' Oh dear, this was terrible. Her eyes strayed to his well-formed biceps and on down to the strong calves of his legs. He had good legs with plenty of muscle definition. She couldn't help noticing these things, she told herself; it was part of the training for her job. Only, she didn't usually experience the added tingle she felt every time she set eyes on him. No, this strange exciting feeling was unique to her encounters with Mike.

They were standing very close to each other. Only a kiss away.

A sudden burst of laughter reached them from beyond the gate and Mike gave a rueful smile. 'My sister, I expect,' he said by way of explanation.

The spell was broken. Kirsty turned towards the car.

'Kirsty.'

She looked back at him and found it impossible to look away. He put out a hand and touched her arm, making it tingle. 'Kirsty,' he said again.

The side-gate clanged as Toby hurtled through it. He pulled up sharp at the sight of her and Mike standing in such close proximity. A tide of heat washed over Kirsty as she sensed his surprise and she took a hurried step back against the side of her car.

'Oh,' said Toby, standing stock-still and staring. 'I just came to say goodbye.'

'I thought I had,' replied Kirsty with a smile. 'But 'goodbye' again, if you like.'

'I know *you* did, but I didn't say 'goodbye' back and I wanted to.'

'OK,' said Mike who'd moved now to stand with an arm round his son's shoulders. 'Now you have. Well done.'

Kirsty said, 'Thanks, Toby, for asking me to come. I've had a great time. I'll see you Wednesday. And I like Buddy — he's lovely.'

Mike was holding Toby in front of him now, in shield-position again. 'Yeah, Buddy's great. Helped us to pick up the pieces, eh Tobes?'

Toby wriggled his shoulders. 'Got to get back — it's my go next.'

'Go on then,' said Mike.

As Toby disappeared into the garden, Kirsty gave a half-laugh. She wasn't sure what had been going to happen then, what Mike had been about to say or do, but it had felt . . . well, special. But special or not, whatever it was, it was lost now.

Just get in the car, she told herself, *out of harm's way, out of temptation. Get in the car and go.*

But she was still having difficulty in tearing her eyes away from Mike's. She groped behind her and felt the smooth metal beneath her fingers, but was still reluctant to look away from Mike's clear grey-green gaze. Where was the car door handle? What kind of idiot couldn't find the handle to a door?

Ah, success! She jerked it open. 'Well.' A quick glance back. 'Thanks again.'

He was still staring at her and once more their eyes locked. He leaned forward. So did she. It was meant to be a quick good-night kiss on the cheek, she was sure it was. Only, somehow it

123

didn't work out that way. Somehow it turned into a full-blown kiss. The sort that shook you to your very core. The sort that went on for a long time, and then left you panting for a repeat performance.

'Oh,' she said eventually, when she was able.

Mike released her shoulders, which Kirsty hadn't even been aware he had been holding until she nearly fell over due to the sudden lack of his support.

'Oh, indeed,' he said, sounding equally shocked.

They stood staring at each other.

Careful, Kirsty, she told herself. *He looks a bit dazed, even more dazed than I feel.*

'Good night, Mike,' she said softly, after a moment when it seemed impossible for either of them to speak. Somehow, she opened the car door fully and slipped inside. Somehow, she managed to start the ignition.

She looked sideways as she turned onto the road and saw that he was still standing exactly where she had left him. He was pulling on his ear with a bemused expression on his face.

* * *

'So the kiss was good then?' asked Jo.

Casting her mind back two days, Kirsty gave what even she knew was a soppy smile. She was glad her phone didn't transmit pictures, because if it could, Jo would crack up.

'Very good. Only . . . '

'Only what?'

'Well, it wasn't exactly pre-planned. It was sort of accidental.'

'All the best kisses are.'

One-handed, Kirsty opened the fridge door and took out a pot of dessert. 'Yes, but does he now regret it?'

Jo raised her eyebrows. 'Do you?'

'Of course not. Crikey — no! But *he* might. He might run a mile thinking I'm after him or something. Thinking — it's too soon.'

'Too soon? How long has it taken?

125

You must be joking.'

'Too soon for him I mean, not me.'

'So what's next?'

'I'm going round there after work on Wednesday. We've only spoken by text. He's got this week off. The kitchens are being built without him. He's bringing Toby to his swimming lesson and he might watch for a bit, I don't know. He's got to go to the aquatic centre to find out about a pond pump or something. Then I'll take Toby home. Mike's going to cook us dinner and show me what they've done on the pond so far.' She took a breath. 'Then on Friday afternoon, I'm going round to help with the pond.'

There was a pause. 'I wouldn't get too excited if I were you. It doesn't sound like the most romantic of dates. Call me old-fashioned if you like, but in my book, first dates usually involve flowers and a bottle of champagne perhaps . . . They say never act with children or dogs. I think that could apply to courting too . . . Not to mention Grandma.'

'Grandma won't be there. She's gone home for the week. Anyway, I like Grandma.'

'You like everyone.'

'No, I don't. I don't like Nina, that's for sure.'

'Nina the Nasty?'

'Hmm. I told you what she said, didn't I?'

'Three times. She's obviously after him. She senses a rival.'

'She's married.'

'So? A little thing like marriage isn't going to stop the Ninas of this world.'

Kirsty shivered. 'I'm just wondering a bit.'

'Wondering what?'

'Whether she's already . . . He's already . . . You know. I mean, four years. It's a long time.'

'Well, what's your gut feeling?'

Her gut feeling? Kirsty thought about it, and shook her head. 'No,' she said. 'I think he's just a bit uneasy around her. Apparently she was Louise's best friend. Although how on earth Toby's mother could have had such shocking bad taste, I can't think.'

'If I were you, I'd bring it up in conversation. Try and find out what's gone on or is going on. It's only fair that you know, after all.'

'I think that's easier said . . . I'll see.'

'Keep me posted then. Oh, here's Paul. Catch up with you later.'

Thoughtfully, Kirsty put down her phone and removed the foil lid from the yoghurt pot. It was caramel, her favourite. Just as she was about to dig her spoon in, she paused. Something about the colour of it brought Nina's cat-like gaze to mind. The caramel-coloured linen dress — that was it. Lovely dress, no denying it. And it looked great on Nina, who was slim to the point of painful, but there was no arguing with the fact that her kind of figure made anything look terrific. Would Kirsty have liked her better if she'd looked a little less terrific? No, not after that warning off.

For a moment she felt gleeful that Nina had felt the need to warn her off. That must mean she felt threatened, mustn't it? She must have sensed that Kirsty and Mike stood a real chance of getting something together.

Kirsty closed her eyes and thought of the kiss again, then dipped her spoon into her dessert and smoothed her tongue over the contents. Mmm, delicious!

* * *

'You like my dad, don't you?'

'Of course I do, Toby. Now come on, one of your legs keeps falling down in the water. I want you to think about both of them working together, just like your arms — they're working beautifully.'

Toby pulled a face but didn't argue. Soon he was swimming a good breast stroke across the pool.

The trouble was, yes, she did like his dad, but Mike had hardly looked at her

129

when he'd dropped Toby off at the pool half an hour ago. He'd just said that he had to rush to check on someone's kitchen but would see them back at the house later. Toby had a key if he wasn't in when they got back, but he definitely wouldn't be long.

Hmm, so Jo was right. It looked as though digging a pond wasn't going to be such a hot date after all. And Mike had been wearing his serious expression again. She might just as well face it; she was on a hiding to nothing here. If one little kiss had frightened him off, maybe he wasn't worth fighting for.

But, she argued with herself, as kisses went it hadn't been a little kiss; it had been a stonking great big one that had started gently and sweetly, building up to a crescendo of heat and fire, and burning passion . . .

It really was hot in here.

'Are you listening to me?' asked Toby. 'I've asked you three times if I can swim along the bottom for a bit.'

Kirsty snapped herself back from

passionate kisses to energetic little boys needing direction. 'One more width showing me your leg movements and you can go under water then for a bit,' she said.

When the lesson was over, Toby insisted on his hot chocolate. Kirsty had changed her top and redone her ponytail and, despite not being too sure what the rest of the day would bring, was eager to take Toby home. This resulted in her rushing her hot chocolate, which for once was very hot indeed, and scalded her tongue.

Mike and Toby's house was quite sizable. Nothing too pretentious, it was a modern build set on a wide plot. There was a larger than normal double-floored garage to one side, and Kirsty remembered that Toby had told her there was a self-contained apartment over the top of it for the au pair. *Very nice too*, she thought. *Wouldn't mind living there myself.*

The main house was comfortable rather than ultra-smart. On the occasions she'd dropped Toby off, Kirsty had only glimpsed the hallway as he had run in. At the barbecue, most of the time had been spent in the garden with occasional forays into the kitchen, which was open and airy with a family room at one end. Now, as she let them in with Toby's key, she discovered through the half-open doors leading off the square hall, that there was a formal lounge at the front of the house and also a large study and a dining room which looked as though it was rarely used.

Unsure quite what she should do, she followed Toby out into the garden and stood next to him, surveying the kidney-shaped excavation in front of them.

'It's big, isn't it?' said Toby proudly. 'We used a digger on Monday. It was wicked, just like what they use on a real building site but a bit smaller. Dad wouldn't let me use it though. I was just allowed to watch.' He broke off and studied the gaping hole in the ground with renewed reverence. 'I didn't think it would be *this* big, but Dad says that once the water and plants are in it'll look much smaller.'

'I expect your dad's right,' agreed Kirsty, wondering when exactly he was going to turn up.

'I'll show you my room, shall I?'

'That'd be good.'

Feeling rather like an intruder, she followed Toby up the stairs. 'This is really cool, Toby,' she said as she walked in. In truth it was much like any other eight-year-old boy's room, decorated in primary colours with bunk beds against one wall, a desk and chair, a small chest of drawers and a fitted cupboard against another.

'I keep my clothes and my stuff in there,' said Toby.

There was a map of the world on the wall and lots of paintings and drawings, obviously crafted by a child's hand, pinned up on a board. On his bedside table was a photo of a smiling lady with straight brown hair and dark eyes just like Toby's.

'That's Mum,' said Toby. 'My dad's told you about my mum, hasn't he?'

Kirsty nodded. 'Thought so . . . He doesn't tell everyone . . . ' confided Toby. 'She was nice.'

Hardly daring to breathe, Kirsty nodded again. 'You have the same eyes,' she said eventually.

Toby looked at her solemnly. 'There's something I have to tell you about my Dad . . . '

★ ★ ★

'Anyone home?' It was Mike.

'We're in the kitchen,' shouted Kirsty, glad that they were by now in the kitchen — where Toby had made himself a peanut butter sandwich, assuring her that he always did so after swimming — and not still in Toby's bedroom, where secrets had been discussed.

As soon as Mike entered the kitchen, Kirsty could see that the relaxed friendly Mike from the barbecue had disappeared. In his place was the efficient Mr Sommerton, who took his duties as a single father very seriously and couldn't think quite why he'd invited his son's swimming teacher to share in the construction of a pond, and — worse still — a meal of his own making. After his first 'Hi there' and a ruffle of Toby's hair, he was cagey almost to the point of being offhand.

'I hope you don't mind eating early,' he said. 'Toby's always famished after swimming, so we eat at about six thirty.'

Toby had disappeared to the television end of the family room, so he was no help. Kirsty swallowed nervously. 'That's absolutely fine.' She watched as he moved around the kitchen, taking salad from the fridge, inspecting and turning some chicken pieces that had been sitting in a marinade, and putting some new potatoes to boil.

'We only eat simple food and I'm no chef,' he said defensively.

'And here was me expecting cordon bleu.'

He gave her a grin. 'I'm sorry, I'm a bit out of practice on the entertaining front.'

135

Suddenly Kirsty felt desperately sorry for him and longed to lean over and stroke the frown line away from his forehead.

'I'm sure whatever we eat will be fine,' she said. 'Toby's shown me the hole in the ground, so I'm itching to know more details later. Meanwhile, is there anything I can do here to help?'

'Toby, come and help Kirsty lay the table,' shouted Mike. 'And when that's done,' he said to Kirsty, 'I think we'll crack open a bottle of wine and have a pre-dinner drink in the way that civilised people do.'

'Great,' said Kirsty. 'I brought some red.'

'Didn't have to do that.'

'Yes, I did.'

'OK.' Mike grinned again and handed her the corkscrew.

Once they each had a glass of wine in their hands, the atmosphere became a little lighter. Leaving the potatoes on a low heat, they wandered outside to survey the pond site.

'I thought rustic-looking paving over-hanging the edge on one side and maybe just grass on the other, as it's to be a wildlife pond.'

'Hmm,' said Kirsty. 'Trouble with grass is, once it gets into your pond it's a nightmare to get out again. How about a few large pebbles or small boulders if you like, so that the birds can splash about in the shallows, and Toby can see the newts and tadpoles swimming around? On the other side of the pebbles you could have a bit of a path joining the existing one, across this bit here say?'

Mike frowned again. 'I'm not sure. I thought a formal edge might make it look a bit too, well — formal, but we'll have to decide before I put the liner in. No good changing my mind after the event. I've got some books inside. Perhaps we'll look at those later, when Toby goes to bed.'

Ah, so there was going to be a 'later'. That sounded promising.

It didn't take long for Mike to turn the chicken in a pan on the hob and soon the spicy smell was circulating in the kitchen, making Kirsty realise that she was quite hungry. They ate their meal at an old pine table and chairs in the kitchen, and talked about Toby's swimming, especially Toby's discovery that swimming underwater was awesome. As an afterthought, Mike mentioned that he had at last obtained a firm order that very afternoon to build and fit a new kitchen.

'It's a whopper,' he said, looking quietly satisfied. 'I've been given carte blanche to do as I want. Well, within limits obviously. The couple are both up to their necks in their own business, and know nothing about building or plumbing or electrics, so it's all down to me. A bit of sub-contracting here and there, but I've got good contacts so that'll be quite smooth. The lady of the house has the final choice on tiles and colour of materials, but we should be able to get started in a month or so.'

'What about our holiday?' asked Toby, swinging his foot against the table leg and blinking rapidly. 'I thought we were going to Devon in the summer holidays? You said so.'

'Yes, we will be,' said Mike. 'Of course we will. That's the great thing. They're away at the same time.'

'I bet there'll be a problem,' said Toby darkly.

'No, there won't, Tobes. Anyway, Saskia's bound to be back by then and Tim and Tracey'll be there with Brad and the others. Who knows, maybe even Sam will come.'

'What about Nina and Jack? Will they be at their cottage?'

'I don't know. Might be,' answered Mike. 'Sounds like a nightmare, doesn't it?' he went on to Kirsty. 'All these people? Thing is, this family place we have near Ilfracombe used to be a small B and B, which makes it a large house really. It's a bit shabby but it's got six bedrooms with en-suites so it's great for holidays. The whole family uses it. Cousins and uncles and aunts and friends. Sometimes we even go there for

Christmas. It's very convenient. Anyway, every year Louise and I used to go along with Tracey and Tim and family, and Sam and my mum, and of course Dad when he was alive. Then, because Nina and Jack like the area so much, they bought a little cottage nearby, and often holiday at the same time as us, so it all worked out rather well.'

Kirsty swallowed her last piece of chicken, which tasted delicious, put down her knife and fork, and took a sip from her wine glass. 'Sounds perfect.'

'Mm.' Mike poured some more wine. 'Are *you* going away this year?'

'No plans at the moment, but usually I go in August when my classes are at their thinnest and the pools are full of school children.'

They'd all but finished their meal and with a look of permission from Mike, Toby got down from the table, taking his plate and cutlery with him to deposit in the dishwasher.

'I'm impressed,' said Kirsty, watching him.

Mike smiled. 'Well, we have to run a tight ship. I know we usually have Saskia, but even so, I expect Toby to pull his weight . . . Tobes, we're going into the garden for a moment to look at the hole — I mean excavation; you want to come?'

Toby shook his head. He was watching something deeply enthralling on the television.

Taking their wine glasses with them, they went out of the French doors and over the grass to the pond site; then, because there wasn't really much to see at this stage, they went on walking round the garden looking at this and that.

'My mother knows the names of all these plants,' said Kirsty. 'I can just about pick out a pansy and a rose.'

'I'm a bit the same,' confessed Mike. 'Louise did all the gardening. Well occasionally I did a bit of digging, but lately I've found a certain satisfaction in keeping it reasonably under control. I think on the whole, though, ponds are

141

more likely to be my kind of thing, and Toby's always wanted one.'

There was a small rose arbour with what Kirsty vaguely remembered her mother telling her was a clematis mixed in with a climbing rose that was just coming into bud. The summer sun was still shafting across the garden, encouraging the half-open roses to give off a hint of musky perfume. They sat down on the seat and finished their wine in an easy silence in the glow of evening sunshine.

Wine and roses, thought Kirsty. *Eat your heart out, Jo!*

Back in the kitchen once more, Kirsty helped with the clearing up, while Mike took Toby up to bed.

'Does he usually go this early?' asked Kirsty when Mike came down again.

'No, only on a swimming night. Did you see him? He could hardly keep his eyes open . . . Oh, I've just picked up a couple of water feature books from the study, if you're interested.'

Well, she'd better be, hadn't she?

Even though sitting outside in the soft evening air with another glass of wine, or even a cup of coffee, just talking and getting to know each other some more would have been preferable. Although sitting side-by-side on the sofa, thighs touching, hands sometimes very near as they pored over the pond books was, in its way, quite stimulating, she found. When — she was sure by accident — their fingers did touch, Mike stared at her for a long moment before jumping up and saying something about how he should have offered her coffee long ago.

He was just so sweet, she thought to herself, watching him as he carefully measured flat spoons of coffee grounds into the cafetiere — just slightly anxious, in the same way as Toby, that he did things correctly. He must have had such a tough time in recent years. Both of them must have.

'I hope this is OK,' he said, bringing the tray of coffee over to the sofa. 'If it's too strong you must tell me.'

'Mike, it'll be fine, honestly. It's only a cup of coffee.'

He gave a sigh as he sat down. 'You must have been so bored this evening. I've been droning on, talking about ponds and my new kitchen order. I'm sorry if I almost sent you to sleep. It's just so nice to talk to an adult about things and my work, now and then.'

'That's all right. I was interested. Anyway, it's not as though you were interrupting anything I had to say. My days are all pretty uneventful and I'm afraid I don't have too much intelligent conversation.' She laughed. 'I'm not exactly the brain of Britain.'

Mike leaned forward. 'Don't say that. Even if you're not, you're good at other things.'

'Such as?'

He looked away and then back again as though determined to say what was on his mind. 'Good with people. Excellent with children. Brilliant with Toby.'

What an unexpected compliment. Kirsty swallowed. 'Oh, bless you for that. Toby's a love.'

'Not all the time,' said Mike with a laugh.

'Underneath he is. He's just finding his way like the rest of us. He's unsure sometimes, but eventually he'll face whatever it is he's scared of.'

Mike's brows drew together. 'What d'you mean, 'scared of'?'

Perhaps that had been a mistake. 'Well, he's a super kid. But there's no denying he's . . . He's . . . anxious, isn't he?'

By now Mike was sitting up very straight and the gap between them had widened considerably. 'I don't know what you mean. He's a well-adjusted child; everybody says so.'

Yes, definitely a wrong move, Kirsty. She shrugged. 'Sorry. I must be wrong then . . . What do I know?'

There was a silence. Mike pushed the coffee plunger down with unnecessary force. 'Anyway, why d'you say 'anxious'?'

'Perhaps it was the wrong word. Perhaps it's just that he's protective of you.'

145

'Of me?' Mike's eyebrows shot up.

'Well, why would you think that's so strange?'

He gave a half-laugh. 'I'm the parent here, remember?'

For a moment Kirsty was silent. Should she say more? Was she betraying a confidence? Then she looked back at Mike's expression and realised how very much he cared for his son. 'D'you remember when you said to me, 'Toby and I, we've picked up the pieces?''

'Well, something like that, yes.'

'D'you know what he said to me today? He said, 'Actually I've picked up the pieces a bit quicker than Dad.''

'He said that?'

Kirsty nodded. 'I know, eight years old and so protective. He was warning me, you see. Not to ask too many questions of you, about his mum. 'Ask me,' he was saying. 'I can handle it. Dad can't.''

Mike cleared his throat and bent over to pour the coffee. 'You're very perceptive.'

'Maybe.' The hand pouring the coffee was surely shaking a little. 'I could also be very wrong. I'm just telling you how I read it, that's all.'

'What d'you think he's scared of then?'

'Perhaps, scared of you being — not happy?'

Mike picked up his coffee and stirred it thoughtfully. 'Well, I'm not unhappy. Not consciously, anyway . . . I worry about Toby. I want to do things right for him.'

Kirsty smiled. 'Oh Mike, you are. Anyone can see that. But a bit more smiling wouldn't come amiss.'

'Right,' he said after a moment longer. 'I'll try to remember.'

So much for trying to help. He looked more anxious now than ever. She searched for something to lighten the mood. 'Did I ever tell you the one about Beethoven's grave?'

The suspicion of a smile hovered at the edges of Mike's lips. 'Oh, go on then.'

'Well, a man visiting the churchyard suddenly noticed that the strains of his ninth symphony were issuing forth from Beethoven's grave. He didn't take much notice, but then on his next visit he recognised notes from his seventh symphony. He drew other grave visitors' attention to it and sure enough they could hear it too. Then the next time he went there he found a large circle of people surrounding Beethoven's grave and there was the sound of the whole orchestra playing his second symphony . . . Just then a gravedigger passed by. 'What's going on here?' asked the man. 'How come all this music is coming from Beethoven's grave?' 'That's easy,' said the gravedigger. 'He's decomposing!'' Kirsty grinned. 'Good eh?'

Mike laughed. 'You are a funny girl, Kirsty.'

Kirsty wrinkled her nose. 'Funny as in 'ha ha' or 'peculiar'?'

His expression became suddenly very still. 'As in 'lovely', actually.'

Nervously, Kirsty licked lips that felt

drier than usual. ' 'Lovely' as in . . . '

Mike leaned forward and tilted her chin. 'No, don't make it into a joke. Lovely as in — you are a lovely person . . . ' he looked at her for a long time. 'Let's just leave it at that . . . For now anyway.'

6

'So, hardly tactful, Kirsty.'

'What?'

'Well, a joke about graves? Wife died four years ago . . . Come on!'

'Oh God! I didn't think.'

Jo's throaty chuckle came down the phone. 'No, I'm sure it was fine. He must have got used to it by now — after all, it *is* four years. You can't not mention death for four years. So, what happened next?'

'Nothing.'

'Nothing? Not even a good-night kiss?'

'Nope. Not even that. I thought there would be when I left. I think it crossed his mind but then well, he just didn't.' Kirsty thought back to that evening, the evening of the Beethoven joke, when he'd called her a lovely person. Something she didn't want to share with anyone, not even Jo.

They'd drunk their coffee in silence until Mike had put down his cup and said quite suddenly, 'Look, I have to take this slowly Kirsty. I'm sorry, but I'm a slow kind of bloke.' His eyes looked searchingly into hers as though he was begging her to understand.

'Because of Toby?'

He nodded. 'And because of me. Because of both of us — and you. I don't want to jeopardize our friendship, or spoil what you have with Toby.'

Slowly, in order to hide the hurt, Kirsty had nodded. 'His swimming's coming on really well,' she said brightly, praying that he wouldn't guess how close to tears she was. 'He's gaining in confidence all the time.' She looked away from him. 'You don't really need me to give him too many more private lessons.'

What on earth was she saying? She risked a glance back at him and glimpsed something close to panic in his eyes. 'I'd really like it if you would,' he said after a moment. 'Carry on, I mean. He enjoys them so much.'

'Right then,' replied Kirsty, quietly relieved.

Not long after that, she'd finished her coffee, and although it was still quite early, looked round for her bag and indicated that she should go. He'd asked her if she was still on for Friday afternoon and she'd said of course she was and why shouldn't she be?

'I'm so glad,' he'd said hesitantly. 'Because I really enjoy your company.'

And because she was soft beyond words, she'd felt comforted by that and told herself that the best things were worth waiting for and she shouldn't be impatient to take their relationship further. Surely it was good that he thought things through? For the moment she would be satisfied with that one spontaneous kiss.

She dragged herself back to the present. 'Another funny thing though. After I left, I was driving home and there was this red car a couple of cars behind me.'

'So?'

'So, I'm almost sure it was Nina's?'

Somehow because the whole idea was, of course, ridiculous, it had come out as a question.

'Really?'

'Well, it might not have been; I mean, I didn't take the number or anything. But you don't see too many red Lotus sports numbers around. It followed me right to my road, before turning off.'

'I think maybe you've got Nina on the brain. Anyway, when are you seeing him again?'

Kirsty laughed to cover the uneasiness she'd felt when she'd thought that maybe Nina was following her. 'You're probably right. I'm getting paranoid . . . Actually, I'm seeing Mike this afternoon, as planned,' she said to Jo.

'More pond-digging?'

'Yeah, I know. I don't expect you to understand.'

'Oh, I understand all right. He's terrified of getting hurt, isn't he? He's using Toby as a chaperone. I think you need to do some serious thinking. This guy's got baggage and he's not really telling you very much, is he?'

'Everyone a day over twenty has baggage these days. And perhaps there's nothing much to tell.'

'I wonder if that makes it better, or worse?'

Kirsty gave an exasperated sigh. 'Jo, you're reading too much into this. I'm just going over there for the afternoon. We'll have a bit of a laugh, that's all.'

Jo gave a sigh. 'That's exactly what I mean.'

$\star$ $\star$ $\star$

Toby was sitting under the kitchen table, playing a silent game on his Nintendo. It was silent because he'd turned the sound off. And he was under the table because, with any luck, neither Grandma nor Dad would spot him there and make him stop with the Nintendo and finish the book he was meant to be reading this week for homework. Somehow his reading had taken a bit of a dive recently, Toby knew that he needed more practice, but he wasn't in the mood for reading now. He was more in the mood for killing things, and it was only a game, wasn't it? He pressed a button and watched as another creature from outer space was obliterated in a satisfying splurge of red and green.

'The thing is, Michael . . . ' Grandma always called his dad Michael. 'The thing is — frankly — it's not much of a date, is it? Girls like her don't grow on trees you know.' Grandma's voice was half-jokey, half-serious, in the same way as when she told Toby it was way past his bedtime. Toby knew that voice, and waited interestedly for Dad's answer.

'Mum, as the Americans say — butt out!'

'I'm only saying.'

'I know what you're saying, and I do like her, of course I do — she's lovely. And well, yes I fancy her, she's eminently fanciable . . . But look, anyone fool enough to take me on has to understand that we come as a package. Toby and me — that's the deal.'

'It hasn't occurred to you, then, that if you go on labouring the point she'll feel as though you're only looking for another au pair but with additional benefits?'

'Mum!'

'All right, I'll say no more. But if you're really serious, take her out somewhere nice . . . without Toby. You know I'll always babysit — not that he's a baby. He's growing into a lovely boy — he's a credit to you and Louise.'

In his crouched position Toby blinked rapidly. Baby? Of course he wasn't a baby!

'Still has nightmares,' said Dad. 'I wish he didn't.'

Grandma's legs, which ended in a pair of ageing sandals, walked within inches of Toby's knees on their way to the kitchen door, where they paused. 'Now, where have I put my shoes? Ah, by the front door . . . ' The sandals turned back towards Toby. 'And Michael, *all* children have nightmares.'

Dad sighed. 'Yes, you're right. Anyway, where is he?' His chair scraped back.

'He should say goodbye to you.'

'Sorry,' said Grandma. 'I'm going to have to go or I'll be late. I'll drop your shopping off later. Anything else to add to the list?'

Dad's feet joined Grandma's before disappearing into the hall. 'Tobes, where are you?' he heard his father shout up the stairs.

Quick as a flash Toby was out from under the table, through the kitchen to the French doors, quickly opening and closing them noisily.

'Oh you were in the garden,' said Dad when Toby reached him halfway down the hall. Toby didn't argue. 'Grandma's going to have her hair done, then she's going on to the supermarket. Anything you can think of?'

'Ice cream,' said Toby. 'Please,' he added, catching Grandma's eye.

* * *

'No, it's all right, Kirsty, I'm not stopping for lunch,' Anne said later. 'I wasn't sure whether you'd have eaten as you were working this morning, so I've put a bag of salad and some smoked salmon in the fridge for you.' Buddy sat with his head on one side. Anne bent to stroke his ears. 'I'm leaving Buddy here while I visit a friend for the weekend. Three boys together.' She gave a twinkly smile.

'Toby'll love that. He thinks the world of Buddy . . . ' Kirsty eyed Anne's neat figure, clothed in casual trousers and a blue striped shirt. 'I hope you have a good time. You look very nice.'

'Thanks. Sometimes the effort seems a bit much, but once you give up, it's a slippery slope down to being a bag lady.'

Kirsty laughed at the very idea of the smart, svelte lady before her turning into a bag lady.

'Oh, you may laugh,' said Anne. 'But when you're getting older and you live alone . . . '

Kirsty smiled, complimented her on

her hair and said again that she hoped she'd enjoy her break. After Anne had left, and Toby had run into the garden with Buddy jumping at his heels, she and Mike stared at each other in what seemed a never-ending silence, until suddenly Mike gestured towards the fridge and said, 'Well?'

Kirsty gave a nervous laugh. 'Oh, I've had a sandwich, thanks.'

'I told Mum you would have done, but she fusses a bit . . . ' He frowned. 'Oh dear, that sounded terrible. Actually, Mum's as good as gold. Doesn't interfere; she's just there when we need her.'

Kirsty nodded. 'Well,' she said, motioning towards her denim shorts and T-shirt. 'I'm here to work, so lead on.'

The June weather had nose-dived into chilly bordering on cold. Maybe shorts hadn't been such a good choice, thought Kirsty. But once she had helped Mike drag the butyl liner into position over the gaping hole that was

159

soon to become a pond, she found she had warmed up considerably.

It was hot work and took a lot longer than any of them had thought. Kirsty had never anticipated that laying a liner could be so complicated, but she was quite content to watch Mike's well-formed torso moving beneath his T shirt as he laboured. Naturally, he did most of the manual stuff, heaving and lifting and patiently reassessing every fold. Toby and Buddy were helpful in holding down corners. Then, at a later stage in the proceedings, Toby was allowed to stand in the middle, in bare feet so as not to damage the liner — although Kirsty personally thought that was taking things a little far — and then to smooth the liner gently into the curves of the edges. 'You've got smaller fingers,' said Mike to his son. 'You can get into all the nooks and crannies.'

'It's better with your socks off,' confided Toby to Kirsty. 'Why don't you come and help?'

So Kirsty took off her deck shoes and helped. She was already feeling slightly dirty and dishevelled, not to mention sticky, when Mike came out with the hose. 'Go easy, Tobes,' he called. 'Not too much stretching of the liner; it's got to stay strong. I think you've done enough now. If you come out, the water will slowly fill it and weight it into all the corners.'

'Can I fill it? Can I?'

'Sure,' said Mike. 'You can fill it. Just don't let Buddy in there. You'd better come out, Kirsty,' he added with a grin. 'Not quite warm enough to paddle.'

Mike leaned a hand over to help her step up from the deepest part of the pond to the shelf where the baskets of water iris and brooklime would be placed. His grip felt strong and firm; her hand in his, safe. It only took a moment for her to step back onto the grass, but she didn't want those few seconds to end.

They stood on the edge of the pond, their hands still linked. Kirsty scarcely

161

dared to breathe. She wondered which one of them would be the first to move away.

'Hi there! Anyone at home?'

The side gateway rattled, and a second later Nina walked through. 'Oh, hi folks, I see you're busy performing horticultural pursuits. How enthralling.' Taking in the hand-holding, yet at the same time managing to indicate that it was too trivial to remark upon, she gave a laugh.

Kirsty snatched her hand away from Mike's, wondering even as she did so why on earth she should care what Nina thought — that in fact it would have been better if she'd left her hand there in Mike's for a further few minutes just to show her! Show her what, exactly, she wasn't sure.

An epitome of confident poise, Nina stepped across the lawn. She was wearing skinny jeans, probably of designer origin, a grey cashmere sweater and lots of immaculate makeup. She looked pretty fantastic, and Kirsty felt a wreck. She put the back of her hand to her cheek, where she just knew there was a streak of mud.

'Oh, you poor thing,' purred Nina. 'You look . . . ' there was a pause and the words 'a mess' hung in the air for a long moment before she finished with, 'exhausted.'

'Well, we've been working pretty hard,' said Mike.

'What are *you* here for?' asked Toby, who'd been staring at her with an expression of disbelief on his face.

'Toby, where are your manners? Nina's a friend. She's just called in to see us,' said Mike, flushing slightly.

'I was just asking,' said Toby in muted but mulish tones. 'That's all.'

'We were going to take a break about now anyway,' went on Mike. 'We'll have a cup of tea, shall we?'

'Lovely,' said Nina, staring hard at Kirsty.

'I'll make it,' Kirsty offered. 'I want to go inside anyway.'

And that was an understatement, she

thought as barefooted she walked across the grass to the kitchen. She dropped her shoes at the door, filled the kettle and turned it on, found mugs and tea bags and lined them all up on a tray, before going to the cloakroom to inspect the dire state of her appearance. And oh dear, it *was* dire, wasn't it? Hair adrift from ponytail, smear of dirt on her nose and cheek, lipstick worn off, mascara smudged. Shakily, Kirsty did her speedy best to repair some of the damage. She made the tea as fast as she could, added a glass of orange on the tray for Toby, and after taking a deep breath, took the tray outside and placed it on the patio table.

She could see Mike gesticulating with his arms, no doubt explaining the approximate location of the plants and where he planned to position a decorative pump trickling water, on the pond's edge. Nina was feigning interest. A rebellious-looking Toby was directing the hose, squirting water into the pond. Buddy was sniffing at nothing in particular.

'Tea up,' called Kirsty brightly. Mike turned and smiled, but just as he was about to walk towards her, Nina took his arm and pointed to something on the other side of the pond. The strategy could hardly have been more obvious if she'd said, 'Oh don't mind Kirsty, she's only the hired help. Couldn't be less noteworthy.'

Toby had glanced quickly over his shoulder and then back again at the water, which was rising steadily in the pond. Mike was now answering Nina's query, whatever that was, but more importantly Nina was still holding his arm.

Kirsty hesitated. Would she look a fool if she called again? She counted silently and slowly to ten. 'Tea!' she called, louder this time. At her call, Toby jerked round suddenly, the hose pipe still in his hand.

With a terrible fascination, Kirsty watched as a jet of water sparkled, arc-like, through the air. There was a high-pitched feminine scream followed closely by a shout of surprised laughter from Mike and Toby. Kirsty put a hand over her mouth. Nina's face and hair were dripping and her cashmere sweater no longer looked quite so elegant. Toby had dropped the hose and was trying to control his giggles.

Although Nina had got the worst of it, Mike had been in the line of fire too. His shirt was soaked, his shorts merely splashed, but he had a wide grin on his face. Nina had a face like a thundercloud — a wet one.

'Sorry,' said Toby in a muffled voice.

'I'll get a towel.' Kirsty fled inside to hide her laughter. Carrying two towels from a folded pile she'd spied in the cloakroom, she came out to find that Nina was no longer as model-like as before. Now she, too, had streaked mascara. In fact, because she used so much of it, it was running down her face in ugly rivulets. It seemed her hair had caught the full force of the jet and now hung in rat's tails around her face, which was still mutinous.

Kirsty derived a wicked sense of

comfort from the sight.

'Oh come on, Nina, it was an accident,' Mike was saying.

'I just turned round,' said Toby. 'That's all. I sort of forgot I was holding the hose.'

Nina grabbed at a towel and attempted a smile, but it was clear she was far from amused. 'Thanks,' she said, dabbing at her hair. 'Of course I know it was an accident. Toby wouldn't do it deliberately, would you Tobes?' She gave him a mock punch on the shoulder. 'I'll go in and sort myself out.'

'I've got a spare top in the car,' said Kirsty hesitantly, because it was obvious the saturated grey one was now useless.

Nina turned the full force of her ice-blue Siamese catlike gaze on her. 'Oh, I don't think so,' she said. 'I'll borrow one of Mike's.' She gave a small laugh. 'We've shared sweaters before.'

'Of course,' said Mike, whose face had gone pink. 'I'll bring you one down.'

'Well, looks like we're the only dry

ones,' commented Kirsty after they'd disappeared into the house together. She watched Toby carefully place the hose at the waterside.

He came and sat beside her on the patio and started swinging his leg against his chair. 'It was funny though, wasn't it?' he whispered. 'Dad thought it was funny, I could tell. I didn't mean her to get quite so wet though.'

It might be best to say nothing now, Kirsty thought. Nothing about it not being an accident; nothing about neither of them liking Nina very much.

About a minute later Mike came back onto the patio. He must have rushed, as he couldn't possibly have spent much time in giving Nina a dry sweater. 'Don't do that again, mate,' he said to Toby. Then he caught Kirsty's eye and they both had to look away in case they laughed out loud.

By the time Nina came out, complete with fresh make-up, newly combed damp hair, and a green sweater that Kirsty was secretly pleased to see did absolutely nothing for her overly made up complexion, Mike was pouring the tea.

'What brings you this way?' he asked Nina, handing her a cup.

'Oh, I was just passing and I remembered that you said you were having a week off with Toby at Whitsun. Jack's in the States — again! I thought I'd call in and see what you guys were doing.'

Yes, and I bet you were just overjoyed, not to mention curious, when you saw my car in the drive, thought Kirsty.

Mike pulled his ear. 'Oh, right. Well, we're just watching the pond fill up now. You've missed all the hard work, I'm afraid. Getting the levels right, and the like. But it's taking shape nicely now. When I've done the edges, another levelling job, and the water's settled itself, we can decide properly on the planting.'

'Interesting,' said Nina, sounding anything but.

Mike laughed. 'It's all right, you don't have to pretend. But you'll be impressed when it's finished.'

'I'm sure,' said Nina.

There was the sound of a doorbell ringing through the house, followed by a frantic barking from Buddy. 'Dad,' called Toby, who'd gone inside for more orange. 'Looks like a delivery.'

Mike got up. 'No peace for the wicked,' he said. 'I wonder if it's the pump I ordered off the internet.'

As soon as he'd gone, Nina turned towards Kirsty and laid an elegant hand, complete with polished red nails, on her arm. 'I'm so glad you're here,' she said, smiling her feline smile. 'I wanted to apologise for the last time we met . . . I'm afraid sometimes, Tracey and Tim, Jack and I, we're a little overly protective of Mike. We're old friends, you see, and we care for him so much . . . ' She looked away and blinked. 'I was elected to see how the land lay with you, and to make it clear we wouldn't stand for any nonsense. Women tend to find him attractive, you see — often the wrong types.' She smiled again out of eyes that were ice blue. 'He's had such a rotten time of it, poor old Mike. Being Louise's closest friend you see, I — we — couldn't bear to see him get hurt again.'

'Oh,' said Kirsty. Then, because she was Kirsty and a trusting person at heart: 'Well, yes I can understand that. But I *am* only a friend, you know. And, for what it's worth, I wouldn't like to hurt anyone either. That's never my intention. But it is four years ago now, isn't it? I should think Mike knows when it's time to move on.'

'Oh, he's come a long way already,' said Nina. 'When I think of the wreck he was. Especially immediately after the event . . . The police gave him such a hard time.'

'Pardon?'

'Oh,' Nina looked surprised. 'You mean he hasn't told you? Not that it makes any difference really, but you see, out of all of us, Mike was the only one without an alibi at the time Louise died. It was only by my saying that I'd got the time wrong and that Mike *was* on the beach when he actually wasn't, that they stopped questioning him.'

Suddenly Kirsty felt slightly sick. 'So you lied for him?'

'Well, if you put it like that.' She shrugged her shoulders as though she'd only just thought of it that way. 'Well, hey, what are friends for?' she asked with another smile.

This time Kirsty didn't smile back. 'But it was an accident,' she said slowly. 'Mike told me it was an accident.'

'Of *course* it was,' said Nina. 'God, you don't think for a moment . . . No, of course, we all *knew* it was an accident.' She looked away for a moment. 'It was naughty to lie, I know that, but I was the only one in a position to do so, right? We all knew Mike could never have harmed Louise . . . I mean, they had their arguments — they were only human after all. But anyone who saw Mike that day would know he was worried and stressed out of his life trying to find her — and when he did, he totally lost it.'

From the kitchen, there was the sound of Toby and Mike talking. Their voices were traveling closer. Nina squeezed Kirsty's arm. 'I'm so glad we got that sorted out,' she said. 'I wouldn't like to feel there was any animosity between us.'

'Oh,' said Kirsty, still reeling from shock. 'No, of course not. Absolutely.'

'Yep, the pump's come,' said Mike, grinning as he stepped onto the patio. 'Looks like it's just the job, hey Tobes?'

'Dad's going to show me how it works.'

'Well, that'll be engrossing no doubt,' said Nina. 'I'm afraid I won't be able to stay for that, Tobes.'

This was news that didn't seem to worry Toby unduly.

Nina stood up. 'Thanks for the tea, Kirsty — oh and thanks for the shower, Tobes. Next time there's a hose around, you'd better watch out — I'll get you back!'

Toby grinned.

Still in a semi-trance, Kirsty gave a half-wave and watched Mike walk Nina out of sight round the side of the house, wondering if he'd kiss her on the cheek before she got into her car and whether Nina would turn this into a hug of a lingering nature, and just what exactly was Nina's game? If it had been to plant seeds of doubt into her mind, Kirsty had a horrible feeling she'd succeeded. Maybe, just maybe, the signs of stress Mike had shown that terrible day on the beach had been because he knew already that Louise was dead in a crevasse at the bottom of a cliff?

She shivered and pushed the thought away.

Mike walked back round the corner of the house with a cheery grin on his face and, as though on cue, the sun came out from behind a cloud.

'Now let's examine the workings of this all-singing, all-dancing, pump,' he said easily.

'Course it's only a reproduction,' said Toby importantly. 'But it's still going to work. We've put a pipe down already for the tube that takes the water from the pond to the pump so it can trickle out again. It'll aerate the water, so it doesn't get too mucky.'

'Crikey,' said Mike with a grin. 'So, he does listen to some of the things I say.'

And despite Nina's obvious opinion that pond-building was nothing short of excruciatingly boring, Kirsty pushed her confusion to the back of her mind and absorbed herself in the process, trying to convince herself that she was glad to be a part of the threesome busy working out where things should go, whether they should put a drain pipe in the bottom for creatures to hide in, should they have pink water lilies or white, and mock cobbles or sandstone flags round the edge of the pond.

And soon she was able to concentrate on the here and now. Thrill a little every time Mike's hands brushed hers, notice the sunlight glance off his thick, springy, silvered hair, which was just so unusual and looked great with the tan he had developed over the last few days. How could she ever have thought he was Toby's granddad? He was so obviously fit; fit and attractive. Just then, as though he felt her eyes on him, he looked up and smiled at her and — oh goodness, she could feel another blush coming on.

Hurriedly, she glanced away and back at the list of bog plants she was meant to be studying.

And as for Nina with her poisonous words and insinuations, well, she just wouldn't let herself think about her. She was just trying to spoil their afternoon, and Kirsty wasn't about to let that happen.

'I'm hungry,' said Toby.

Mike looked at his watch. 'Six o'clock, no wonder,' he said. 'How about we walk over to the pub for an earlybird meal?'

'Well, I'll need to clean up a bit.'

Mike leaned over and flicked a spot of mud from her nose. 'Only a bit,' he said. 'Anyway, we have a shower, and you don't need to look posh for a pub.'

'I've got a clean top and some crops in the car,' went on Kirsty, hoping she didn't sound too eager.

'What're crops?' asked Toby.

'Short trousers,' said Kirsty. 'A cross between shorts and trousers.'

'They should be called shrousers then, or torts.' He gave a giggle.

'Very good,' said Kirsty. 'I'll fetch them and change in the cloakroom, shall I?'

After they'd smartened themselves a little, they strolled in a leisurely fashion to the pub, which was ten minutes away and had a garden at the back, so Buddy was allowed too. As they walked they chatted easily enough, but at the back of Kirsty's mind was the niggling piece of knowledge so subtly implanted by Nina that in reality, Mike had had no alibi for the time of his wife's accident. The awareness of that fact made her feel uncomfortable, and she knew that before the relationship could be taken any further she would have to ask Mike more about Louise's death.

But not now, certainly not now with Toby marching along in front of them occasionally taking a longer stride in order to avoid treading on a crack in the pavement. Not now, while the sun was shining and somehow her hand had found its way into Mike's.

By the time they reached the pub, the air was cooler but the sun was still showing itself. It was still before seven, and the garden was all but empty. They found a table that wasn't too sticky, decided on what to eat, and Mike went inside to order.

'He doesn't usually let me have beef burgers because he's not sure what's in them, but he is tonight because you've ordered one too,' said Toby happily.

'Well, they're not my staple diet, but it doesn't hurt to have one now and then.'

'What's 'staple' mean?'

'It means the thing you eat the most of.'

'Oh,' said Toby. Then, 'You haven't told me any jokes lately.'

Kirsty grinned. 'OK. Just so happens I heard one the other day that I thought you might like. There's this teacher and she says to Johnny, 'If I give you two cats and Abby gives you two cats and Ben gives you two cats, how many cats will you have?' Johnny thinks for a minute, then he says, 'Seven.' The teacher says, 'No. Now think about it. If I give you two apples and Abby gives you two apples and Ben gives you two apples, how many apples will you have?' 'Six,' says Johnny. 'Very good,' says the teacher. 'Now then, if I give you two sweets and Abby gives you two sweets and Ben gives you two sweets, how many sweets will you have altogether?' 'Easy, peasy,' says Johnny. 'Six.' 'Right,' says the teacher. 'Very good indeed, Johnny. Now you're getting the idea. So, if I give you two cats, Abby gives you two cats and Ben gives you two cats, how many cats will you have?' 'Seven,' says Johnny. Well, by now the teacher's exasperated — that means fed up, Toby. 'How do you make it seven?' she says. 'That's easy,' says Johnny. 'I already have a cat at home!''

Kirsty watched as the joke caught up with Toby and a grin of comprehension split his face. 'Oh, I see,' he said. 'He could do it all the time. He was having his teacher on, wasn't he?'

'Yep,' said Kirsty.

'That's good,' he said. 'I'll try it on Dad later.'

'Yes, make it later when I'm not here, or I might laugh and give the game away. Best way to tell it is as though it happened at school. One of your classmates or something.'

'Yeah, cool,' said Toby, his eyes lighting up at the thought.

Mike came back carrying a beer, a glass of wine and a glass of orange.

'Dad,' said Toby almost before he sat down. 'I must tell you about something that happened at school . . . '

Kirsty smiled behind her hand. Oh well, what did she expect? Toby was grinning all over his face. She watched as Mike's face lit up too, and suddenly found her heart lurching at the sight of the two of them, who in such a short time had come to mean so very much to her, sharing an old joke that hardly warranted so much hilarity.

Be careful, Kirsty, she warned herself, *you're getting in too deep. It's not only Mike who can get hurt here.*

7

'But how much longer?' asked Toby, blinking rapidly.

Dad looked at him and then quickly away again, so Toby knew the answer wasn't going to be good. 'Until the middle of August,' he said.

'Oh,' said Toby. 'So we won't be able to go to Devon.'

Dad gave a smile. 'Did I say that? No, I didn't! Of course we'll still go to Devon. It's just that Saskia's mother has had an operation and Saskia doesn't want to leave her until she's well again. We'll still go on holiday. Nothing to stop us.'

'But Grandma's going on a cruise so *she* can't come with us either — she said it would dovetail nicely. I remember because I asked her what 'dovetail' meant and she said . . . '

Dad grinned and took hold of Toby by the shoulder. 'I know what 'dovetail' means, Toby. We'll be fine without Grandma. Tim and Tracey are coming; you'll hardly miss Saskia.'

'She would've liked to have come,' said Toby stubbornly.

Toby's dad kept his eyes on him. 'Well, anyway, you've got homework to do and I've got some calls to make. I just thought I'd tell you about Saskia so you could get used to the idea.'

Toby kicked the table leg and looked at the maths sheet in front of him. It was full of questions where you had to fill in the blank spaces. Huh, as if he didn't know what you had to add to eight to make fourteen! He picked up his pencil.

The trouble was, Toby had been feeling a bit strange lately. A bit as though he'd forgotten something but he wasn't quite sure what the something was. Sometimes he found himself looking for something, then wondering what it was he was searching for. Every morning when he woke up, he looked intently at the photo he had of Mum and tried hard to remember what she had smelled like; how, when she'd looked at him with her dark eyes creasing to a smile, he'd felt warm and happy inside. Then he would shut his eyes and recall the small patch of eyebrow just above the bridge of her nose which grew in the wrong direction, and he'd glance in the mirror to reassure himself that his eyebrow still did exactly the same thing. It made him feel better somehow.

To recall the sound of her laugh and the perfume of her skin was more difficult though. Grandma had given him one of his Mum's favourite scarves, which for a long time he used to keep under his pillow until one day he'd decided it would be better nestling in a drawer with his socks. But from time to time he'd retrieve it and hold it next to his cheek in order to reassure himself that it was still safe and not forgotten.

He'd grown very fond of Saskia and it was a shame she wasn't coming back in time to come to Devon. Since she'd been accompanying them, the holiday had become very different from the old family holidays when Mum was still with them. Saskia was the very opposite of Mum, who liked to take long walks and examine every shell and piece of driftwood. Saskia preferred to organise games on the beach, and sometimes they even lit a bonfire and they'd all sit round while she tried to teach them Polish songs. Not that he hadn't enjoyed the holidays before, but he wouldn't have liked to try to replicate them exactly, without Mum. Somehow that wouldn't have felt right.

Toby filled in the answer to one of his sums.

But still, Tracey and Tim were coming, and that meant Brad and Rosie — and of course Jenny, who would probably try to boss them about, would be there too. So it would be OK. He put down his pencil; he needed his fingers for the next sum. One, two, three, four, five. He stopped with his little finger poised on the table top, an expression of dismay on his face. He'd forgotten about Nina. Would she and Jack be there? Would they be at their cottage, which, as Mum had always said, was near — but not *too* near? He hoped not. He wasn't sure he could deal with Nina without Saskia or Grandma or Sam there as backup.

Toby didn't really know why everyone kept saying Nina used to be Mum's best friend. Perhaps it was just because they used to go to school together. Toby always thought of his dad as being his mum's best friend, with Nina skulking somewhere on the edges trying to gain entry. But Mum had said Nina was unhappy because she didn't have any children and that was why Toby had to be especially nice to her.

On that thought, Toby's mind froze. There was something very wrong with that. Surely, Mum had changed her mind? And suddenly Mum's voice, with that familiar little catch in it, came through to him as clear as clear could be. *'You can't have him, Nina. Not him, or his* son. *Not even his sweater.*' For a moment he even imagined he could smell the sea air, feel the sea breeze on his face.

Sweater, sweater, sweater.

Half-forgotten images swirled round in his brain.

Toby kept his head very still, but swivelled his eyes in their sockets to take in the familiar contours of the kitchen. No, there was only Buddy who, head on one side, was looking at him enquiringly, and then there was just himself and his maths homework. Dad was in his study making a call; he could hear his deep, yet soft tones as he spoke into his phone. Grandma was in the front room watching her favourite soap, and there was no one else here.

He was getting muddled — that was it. Like sometimes when he woke up in the night not knowing where he was. It was like a dream. An awake dream, probably because Nina borrowed Dad's sweater after he'd accidentally-on-purpose turned the hose on her — and that had been funny, hadn't it?

He gave a weak smile and thought he'd just pop along the hallway and finish his maths with Grandma; he didn't like to think of her being lonely.

* * *

Even though it was mid-July now, the summer was still deciding in its fickle way whether or not to give Britain a miss this year. And Kirsty now had even more reason to ask Mike more about Louise's accident, but hadn't decided upon the best time to do so. She was also delaying paying her mother a long overdue visit and telling her about Mike. Of the two options, visiting her mother seemed the easier.

Since leaving home, Kirsty had kept her phone calls regular but her return visits minimal, a situation that suited both parties. Thirty-one, Kirsty felt, was quite time enough for her to, if not exactly cut, then certainly loosen the family ties. But now, quite unexpectedly, she felt the urge to tell her mother about Mike.

Slightly disconcerted, because she'd never felt this desire to confide in her mother before, she thought again about why this might be. She acknowledged with a sigh that her attachment to Mike and Toby and even Grandma was, instead of wearing off, becoming deeper and more integral to her life. Despite Mike's undoubted baggage and the mysteries about Louise's death, the idea of ending it had gradually become unthinkable.

When she wasn't with him, Kirsty struggled to pinpoint what exactly it was about Mike that made her heart race and a silent longing take over every sense in her body. What it was about a certain little boy, with his way of anxiously considering things before voicing a statement, his fascination with words and their meanings, that made her want to ruffle his hair and tell him a joke to banish the apprehensive expression that was always hovering behind his eyes.

'It's all very well, Kirsty, but where is this leading?' Jo asked her on more than one occasion. 'You have a future too, you know.'

'I can wait,' Kirsty would reply. 'Good things are worth waiting for. I'm in no rush.'

Jo's only answer would be a sceptically raised eyebrow.

On swimming nights, it had become a habit for Kirsty to drive Toby home and share their evening meal. It was good, she thought, that they could happily spend the evening together, watch a film, or just sit and talk until Kirsty decided to leave. Mike would give her a hug and a kiss on the cheek, then he'd walk to the car with her and they'd kiss again; and even though Kirsty knew — she just knew — they both wanted to take the kiss further, she also understood that this was the very reason there were no kisses inside the house on the sofa, where things might get out of hand. Sometimes she tried to convince herself that it made a pleasant change to be courted, if a courtship was what it was, in this gentlemanly fashion. At other times she'd arrive home in a frustration of impatience, wondering why on earth she was wasting her time with Mike, as he couldn't possibly care for her in the least to be content with so little.

They'd been out without Toby on a few, what Jo might call 'dates'. Mentally, Kirsty ticked the occasions off. They'd been to the cinema twice — well, three times if you counted the time they took Toby. But when they'd gone for an Italian meal it had been just the two of them. They'd also driven, un-chaperoned for once, to a 'shabby genteel' hotel near Christchurch, where they'd had lunch and the waitresses were garbed in black complete with white lace-trimmed pinnies.

'Lovely place,' Mike had said. 'Best English food for miles. It's like stepping back fifty years or so.'

Then he'd surprised her by taking her to a jazz concert, where he'd unwound with the music and closed his eyes in enjoyment as he'd listened to a talented sax player squeezing emotion from every note of a blues number, responding with enthusiastic applause at the end. Totally beguiled at this unexpected unleashing of a passion he normally hid so well, Kirsty had paid more attention to watching him than she had to the music; and when he'd taken her hand in his, she'd felt a shared happiness that threatened to overwhelm her.

On another occasion they'd been invited to Tracey and Tim's home for supper. Their home proved to be large and welcoming but, because it needed renovating, was in a continual state of upheaval. After the children had gone to bed — Toby quite excited to be sharing Brad's room for the night — the adults had sat round an old mahogany Victorian dining table, consuming a goulash of gigantic proportions along with some garlic bread and plenty of red wine.

It had been a fun, relaxing evening, sitting in the shadows of the flickering candlelight, ignoring the awful old wall paper that was peeling off the walls, relishing instead the homely feeling of camaraderie that the room exuded. Kirsty had warmed to them both, first meeting them at the barbecue, and to her relief found that on a second meeting Tracey and Tim were as friendly and down-to-earth as ever and felt she'd been accepted at least by some of Mike's friends.

But the evening had to end. After peeking into the room Toby was sharing with Brad, Mike indicated that he would drive Kirsty to her flat, before going on to his own home. He'd pick Toby up in the morning, he said. Kirsty, wondering if there was any significance in the exchanged glance between Tim and Tracey, felt an excited shiver travel down her spine.

'Thanks for such a lovely time,' she said as they prepared to leave.

'You must come again,' said Tracey. 'You'll always be welcome. It's lovely to have these evenings with old friends.

What with the house and the kids, we don't really get out very much so all our entertaining's at home.'

'It was lovely,' said Kirsty again.

Once in the car, she stole a glance at Mike's face. Oh dear, he looked rather forbidding — or was it tension that was giving his mouth that firm, thin look?

She gave a low chuckle. She couldn't help herself.

Immediately, Mike turned towards her and his mouth relaxed to its normal fullness. 'What's so funny?'

'Nothing. Well, actually — you are.'

He grinned. 'Why?'

'I'm not going to eat you, Mike.'

'I know.'

'OK, then. Chill, why don't you?'

He pulled a wry face. 'Too much work, I suppose. Not enough relaxation.'

'Sometimes, Mike, you just have to give yourself to the moment.'

Mike fiddled with the dashboard and the car was suddenly filled with the smooth tones of Michael Buble proclaiming the strength of his love.

Mike cleared his throat. 'It's just the radio station,' he said, starting the engine and putting it in gear.

'Don't apologise. I love Michael Buble . . . ' Kirsty hummed a few bars along with him. 'They're very good friends aren't they?'

He glanced sideways at her. 'Tracey and Tim? The best. I'm very lucky indeed to have them.'

'Well, perhaps they're lucky to have you too. Tracey told me you designed and installed their kitchen for free and got some really good deals on the units.'

Mike pulled at his ear. 'She shouldn't have told you that. You'll be wanting me to do your kitchen next.'

She cleared her throat. 'Well, it's a thought. I've never shown you my kitchen, have I? You're usually in such a rush, either picking me up or dropping me off. You never seem to have time to come in . . . You can see it tonight if you like. D'you want to come up for coffee?' She held her breath. *Say yes*, she thought, *please say yes*.

There was a silence that was probably only small, but felt like forever to Kirsty.

'Sounds good,' said Mike, not taking his eyes off the road.

She didn't dare to answer.

By the time they pulled up outside Kirsty's flat, the anticipation was causing her heart to hammer painfully against her ribs. She stole another glance at him. His expression was serious. He turned the ignition off and sat a moment longer, examining at the keys in his hand as though he'd never set eyes on them before.

On impulse Kirsty leaned over and kissed him on the cheek. His eyes darkened but were unfathomable as he turned towards her. A groan came from the back of his throat as he pulled her to him.

He was such a good kisser.

But this time there was a searching need to his kiss that left her breathless with desire. She felt an answering need stir within her, and found that the power to think had all but deserted her.

She gave another shudder and attempted to break away. But with even more urgency Mike pulled her towards him again. This was it. The time was right. They would go in now, up the stairs to her flat where they'd have the privacy to explore their love further. A small sigh of pleasure escaped her as she found herself melting into another kiss. Then suddenly, almost roughly, he wrenched away from her.

'I — I don't think I'll come up. I'm sorry. It's — it's not such a good idea.'

Feeling as if she'd been smacked hard in the face, Kirsty sat as though she'd been carved out of stone. How could he kiss her and hold her, as though he wanted her more than anything else in the world, at the same time as turning down her open invitation to come closer? Angry, disappointed tears pricked at the corner of her eyes. The misery that threatened to overcome her was almost unbearable.

'I suppose you're still in love with Louise?'

It had come out as a whisper. Horrified, she caught her breath. How could she have said such a thing?

Mike had frozen into his seat.

'I'm sorry,' she said. 'I should never have said that. Obviously, it must take ages . . . '

Mike sighed. 'No, it's me who should be sorry . . . I had no business to do that, get so carried away . . . It's just you're so very, lovely, so sweet.' He stopped, then went on haltingly. 'You're the best thing that's happened to me in a long, long time. I'm . . . I don't know, unprepared, I suppose you'd call it. Unprepared for . . . ' he gestured around him. 'All this . . . I've been so *focused*. I know it's overused, but in this case it's true. I'm focused on giving Toby a good start. Well, he's had a lousy start. Losing your mother at four years of age can't be good, I recognise that. But, OK then, a fresh start. I'm focused on that. That, and the business, so that he'll have a good future.' He sighed again and rubbed his forehead. 'People

say you must move on . . . If I had a
pound for every time that's been said
. . . But, Louise left a huge gap in our
lives . . . It takes time. And sometimes,
you just don't want to move on.
Nobody tells you — move on to what?
So when something creeps up on you, it
gives you a sort of shock.'

Kirsty swallowed. Her heart went out
to him. He looked so lonely and so
vulnerable sitting there staring at the
windscreen as though he expected to
see only bleakness ahead. She drew a
shaky breath. 'I'm trying to understand,
Mike. But I'm not a threat, honestly.
Don't shut me out. Look, if a little light
flirtation is all you want . . . ' she
shrugged. 'A few kisses never hurt
anyone, did they?' To her annoyance,
her last words came out on a tremble.

Mike turned to her with concern in
his eyes. 'Oh God,' he said. 'I'm sorry.
I've upset you, haven't I? Of course I
have. I'm hopeless.' He looked devas-
tated. 'I'm such an idiot . . . Oh, come
here.' His arms were round her again,

comforting this time, and it was all right. Smelling the by-now familiar scent of his aftershave, she sniffed with relief into his navy sweater. Even if he wasn't going to accept the invitation; even though this was just a good-night hug and kiss, he wasn't going to tell her it had all been a terrible mistake, after all. It was all right.

Or *almost* all right, Kirsty thought to herself later, lying in her lonely double bed. It was almost all right, because he'd told her slowly, haltingly that he was very, very fond of her. Too fond of her, he said, to ever want to hurt her. There were things he wanted to tell her about. Things he owed it to her to make clear. Only now wasn't the time. He knew he wasn't being fair — he should never have become so involved; he hadn't been able to help himself. But he valued her friendship far too much to ever risk losing it.

And she'd said that she understood; that it didn't matter. That she was happy with the way things were; that when she'd asked him up for coffee — that was all she'd meant really.

What a liar, she thought, turning over and trying to find a cool place on the pillow. She'd wanted more, so much more than that.

Thinking of this now, over a week later, she wasn't so sure. What about *her*? What about her needs? She was thirty-one years old; did he think she'd come through life unscathed? What about her heart? Did he ever consider that her heart might also have been bruised a few times? If this was only going to be a light flirtation, what would *she* have when it ended?

Nothing!

Mike had a good circle of friends, his lovely home, a business that was thriving and all-absorbing and, most of all, he would still have Toby. Didn't he realise that if the flirtation were to escalate into something more, and that something more ended badly, she would have as much to lose as he would?

Kirsty sighed. Not because the

evening, including the good-night kiss, hadn't been lovely — because it had; but because since then, although Mike had been friendly — texting her, sharing supper with her on swimming night — he still hadn't expanded on just why he was keeping her at arm's length, and her imagination was telling her that the something that was stopping him was not a some*thing*, but a some*one*.

And that someone had to be Nina.

Maybe Jo was right. Four years was a long time. Before Louise's death, Nina was already his friend. It seemed she'd been Louise's closest friend. Maybe, Nina had made herself available and they'd turned to each other for comfort and Nina didn't want that particular form of comfort to end. Goodness knew her husband Jack never seemed to be around. Possibly, Mike and she had been conducting an affair.

Maybe they still were!

After all, Nina was stunningly attractive, and also canny enough never to show any man in whom she was interested her evil side.

At any rate, whether it had never been, was over, or was still going on — the time for explanations was now long overdue.

* * *

'Darling, you look . . . ' Her mother paused and held Kirsty away from her on the doorstep. 'Different . . . Now, what is it?'

Kirsty shrugged. 'Search me.'

'It's your hair. It's longer, isn't it? And it looks a bit blonder. Suits you.'

'Yeah. Just had the roots done.'

'And — no pink!'

'I wondered when you'd spot that. It sort of washed out.'

'What happened?'

'Thought maybe it was time to stop rebelling.'

'Rebelling?'

'Yes, I thought that perhaps, going out with . . . Oh, hark at me, I sound

Victorian . . . The thing is, Mum . . . '
Suddenly the words came out in a rush.
'I'm seeing someone. He's very nice.
His wife died four years ago, and he has
a young son. And well, I don't know
what's going to happen, but I thought I
should tell you.'

Kirsty's mum took a step back into
the hall. 'And he doesn't approve of
pink hair?' she asked, sounding quite
defensive on her daughter's behalf.

Kirsty blinked with surprise. She'd
always thought her mum considered
pink hair was a little bit, well, not quite
what she would expect from a daughter
of hers. 'No, no. Nothing like that. I
think he quite likes it; he likes it loose
too. It's not that important really. I just
. . . well, Mum, I really like him. And
Toby — that's his eight-year-old son;
he's one of my swimming pupils — I
really like him, too.'

'Well, come in, darling. I'll make
some tea and you can tell me about it.'

Kirsty followed her mother through
the hall out to the untidy kitchen at the

back. She could smell a chicken roasting and saw the half-prepared vegetables on the counter. She wondered if there might be enough for one more serving.

'You'll stay for dinner, of course?'

'Great,' said Kirsty. 'Love to. Feel like I haven't seen you for ages.'

'That's because you haven't. I've called a few times, but all I've had back is, 'I'm fine, Mum, just busy. Catch you later.' But we'll forgive you, because you sounded happy and,' she stopped and gave Kirsty another scrutinising look, 'you look happy too.' She filled the kettle at the sink. 'So what's his name? How old is he? Where does he live? He's not smothered in tattoos, is he?'

Guiltily thinking of the small flower tattoo she'd put under her right shoulder blade two years ago, Kirsty laughed. 'No — at least, I don't think so.' Then she blushed, thinking how ridiculous it was that her mother could still make her blush. 'I'd like you to meet him. I think you'd like him. His mother's really nice.'

'Oh? So you've met his mother?'

'Well yes, early on, actually. She doesn't live with them but looks after Toby a lot because Saskia — she's the au pair — has had to go back to Poland because her mother's ill. Anyway, Anne — that's Mike's mum — she sometimes stays there . . . Only you see, the thing is, Saskia won't be coming back now until the middle of August, and that means when they go to Devon there'll be a spare room, so Mike asked me, only yesterday actually, if I'd like to go with them . . . '

'Stop, stop, stop,' said Kirsty's mum. 'Wait while I pour out the tea, then start again at the beginning and let's see if I can make any sense out of it. And oh, darling, it's lovely to see you looking so well, and so happy. I'm thrilled, really I am. Now sit down and tell me all about it.'

★ ★ ★

She'd been right to make the visit home, Kirsty thought later. Mum had been fine with the idea of a man with a past, fine with the whole concept of her going away with him and his son and his friends. Of course, there was no reason why she shouldn't be, Kirsty told herself. After all, she was thirty-one now. She was probably mad to think she needed her family's approval on her lifestyle; but somehow with Mike, it was important to her that they liked him in a way it had never been with any previous boyfriends.

Encouraged by her mother's reaction, Kirsty lost no time in pouring her heart and her doubts out to Jo.

'Maybe he has a reason for not telling you every little thing.' Jo said.

'Jo, he's told me nothing,' Kirsty replied.

'Yes he has,' her friend went on, after a pause. 'He's given you the bare bones. He probably doesn't want to dwell on it . . . Look, I warned you this wasn't going to be easy. The guy has baggage.

Remember? But you obviously think he's worth it . . . It's Nina that's bugging you, isn't it? And that's precisely what she intended.'

Kirsty didn't tell her that twice now she'd thought Nina's car had been behind her on her way home. She didn't tell her because she didn't want to be accused of being paranoid and, conversely, wanted Jo to take her suspicions seriously.

So when Toby had announced that Saskia wasn't coming back until mid-August, Kirsty, who yet again had talked herself out of any immediate form of confrontation with Mike, only wondered when, if ever, she was going to get Mike to herself for even a little time. Then she chastised herself for being selfish and impatient, and . . . waited.

This time, though, the waiting had paid off, because three days later Mike had taken the wind from her sails by nervously asking her if she would consider coming with them to Devon. 'You'd have your own room,' he'd said when she didn't answer immediately. 'I want you to be sure on that. I thought that, seeing as you have no holiday planned and you said August would be good . . . Well, it seemed silly not to ask you, when Tim and Tracey like you so much and we'd all enjoy your company. Also, it would give us time to be together to talk. For you to understand — about our life, about Louise. Everything!' His expression for a moment had been almost pleading. But Kirsty hardened her heart. Why hadn't he said that *he* couldn't bear to be without her, that it was *he* who wanted her company, not just his friends, or Toby? Because while it was very nice, very flattering, to know she was liked, she wanted *Mike* to like her; no, more than that — to feel passionate enough about her to forget everything and everyone else, in the same way she felt about him.

So, she'd asked, could she think about it? She wasn't sure whether she might do something with her family, but she was visiting her mum shortly in order to discuss holiday plans. Mike's face had closed up. 'Yes, of course,' he'd said. 'We mustn't monopolise your time.' And there it was — that terrible 'we' again.

But now, she'd visited Mum, and she'd spoken to Jo. She no longer had a reason to put off asking Mike what exactly had happened four years ago, and what Nina had to do with any of it. Once again she'd strengthened her resolve, and this time she'd made it clear that she wanted to understand, before embarking on a trip to Devon with them, just exactly what the history was. She needed to know and recognised she would never have a better opportunity.

So, now she faced him across a corner table in The Queen's Head, the very same pub they had visited on their first date. *If you could call it a date*, she thought to herself glumly. But date or not, tonight she'd made a special effort with her appearance. Her hair fell loose to her shoulders in the way he liked it;

she was wearing jeans and a duck-egg-blue top that he'd admired on her before. She'd also paid careful attention to her make-up, which was light but gave her the confidence of knowing that she looked her best.

On the table between them were two glasses of white wine. Her mouth felt dry. She took a sip.

'OK, fire away,' said Mike with a smile that didn't quite cover his anxiety.

'It's not the inquisition, Mike, but you must realise that there are things I want to know about Louise's accident.'

'Sure,' said Mike, but she noticed a nerve working in his cheek.

'So, why don't you just tell me about it — all of it?'

Mike looked away from her. 'You might despise me.'

Kirsty blinked with surprise. 'Despise you? Now why on earth should I do that?'

'Because, well . . . ' He met her eyes squarely. 'That morning, the morning of the accident, we'd had a row. Not a terrible row. But a row, nonetheless. One that Toby heard and Tracey and Tim could hardly not have heard, as we were all in the same house.'

A row about Nina? Kirsty wondered. She licked her lips. 'What kind of a row?'

'Oh, nothing much. I was spending too much time at work. I hardly saw her and Toby. You know the sort of thing . . . She had cause to be annoyed. I *was* spending too much time at work, trying to get the books to balance, trying to get new business . . . I'd taken my mobile and my laptop to Devon. The laptop in particular annoyed her.' He sighed. 'She didn't understand. Having your own business takes over everything — it's never-ending.'

Kirsty nodded.

'Louise could be a bit excitable. Sometimes she could get carried away . . . She accused me of having an affair.'

She shivered. The wineglass in her hand was ice-cold; it must have been in the fridge. She didn't think they did that in a pub. Absently, she shifted it in her fingers. She felt slightly sick. 'And were you?' she asked, surprised at how steady her voice was. 'Were you having an affair behind your wife's back?'

There was a long, empty silence.

8

Mike's shocked eyes met hers. 'No, of course not . . . I was married. I'd never do anything to hurt our marriage. Anyway, I loved Louise. Of course I wasn't having an affair!'

Immediately Kirsty felt contrite. 'I'm sorry,' she said with relief. 'I had to ask.'

Their gazes held for a long moment. His grey-green eyes were free from guile. 'Well, I wasn't having an affair, and I think Louise knew that quite well. She was just trying to bring home to me how much I was neglecting her and Toby. And she was right, I was spending too much time on the business . . . God knows, I had plenty of time to reflect on that afterwards. I suppose my priorities had become a bit skewed. We had a heavy mortgage, and small businesses take a lot of looking after in a recession. Anyway, I'm not making excuses, just telling you what the row was about.'

Kirsty nodded.

'It was one of those misty mornings,' went on Mike. 'Devon is well known for them. Sometimes the mist clears; often it doesn't. We were all going to meet up with Nina and Jack on the beach late that morning. Having breakfast and getting the kids ready and the beach gear always took a major chunk of time. Although the row was over, Louise was still a bit subdued and we were on the quiet side, I suppose. Most of our remarks went via Toby, who was at the verbal stage and was prattling on between the two of us. But Tim and Tracey lightened the atmosphere and the kids all mucked in together. We parked at the small, little-known car park at the top of the cliffs; all it consists of is a patch of shingle hidden from the old coast road, with a rather antiquated toilet. There's only room for about six cars, so a new, improved car park has been built further along the coastline where there's a larger bay,

215

complete with a café with tables and chairs; much more attractive and popular. But the little bay where we used to go is more private, and we liked it — so, on that particular day, that's where we went. As usual, we made our way down the path to the beach, carrying our stuff with us. The boys ran ahead and Jenny helped Rosie over the tricky bits. It's not a dangerous path, but steep in places and quite long. Further along the cliff is dangerous, however, and you have to take care there, as we all knew well . . . '

For a moment Mike put his head in his hands and rubbed at his forehead. 'Once we arrived at the beach, I'm afraid it all gets a bit woolly. We'd done the same thing so many times before, you see. I wish I could remember, but I can't. Even immediately afterwards I couldn't remember with any real clarity — I suppose it was the shock. And as for now — well, my memory's even worse, just a jumble of what other people have told me happened . . . I know, for example, that we'd brought some rolls and a couple of flasks of coffee with us, and we must have eaten and drunk at some point . . . It was chilly at first, but then the sun broke through the clouds and we thought we'd be in for a good day. Eventually Jack and Nina turned up, I suppose, and Nina would have been impossibly made up as usual — it always surprised me that she bothered to come to the beach; I've never seen her go in for a swim — but Jack's a strong swimmer and loved swimming, really loved it, and would go in the water whatever the weather and stay out for hours.

'I was pretty tired and, what with the argument that morning, not feeling terribly sociable, so I just lay back and closed my eyes . . . Apparently Rosie started playing up a bit, saying she was hungry, so Tracey and Tim decided to walk the kids further down the beach through the rock pools to the next beach and the café. At the thought of chips, Toby was going to go with them, but at the last minute he changed his mind and came running back. I told Tracey not to worry, that I'd dig him a sand castle, but somehow I must have drifted off to sleep before I got round to it . . . I do vaguely remember Louise saying she'd take Toby up on the cliffs for a walk. I nearly offered to go with them, but felt Louise was still being edgy, so I didn't . . . I fell asleep instead.' He stopped talking and his eyes darkened. 'And that was the last time I saw my wife alive . . . Walking down the beach, in a pink T-shirt and denim shorts, holding Toby's hand . . . We didn't even say goodbye — it was just 'see you later', which of course, I never did.'

Mike expelled a shuddering breath, and took a moment before going on in a more even tone. 'When I woke up, the sun had gone in and it was chilly and grey. I remember looking round but it seemed like I was alone. I think I walked down to the shoreline and could just about make out Jack's head in the sea. Good luck to him, I thought. I certainly didn't fancy a swim. I needed the loo, was feeling cold, and couldn't find my sweater. As I told the police, those are the things I remember. There was no sign of any of the others coming back, so I put on my sandals and made my way back up the cliff path to the awful old loos at the top. About halfway up, there's a shelf of rock where I stopped and checked my mobile, which was in my shorts pocket. You can get a signal up there; you can't always get one on the beach. There were a couple of missed calls. Feeling guilty — because this was, after all, meant to be a family holiday and I shouldn't be taking calls — I returned one of them. The call lasted a while, then I went on up, used the loo and . . . ' His voice petered out and his eyes clouded with thought. 'Yes, I remember that. I remember standing at the top and looking out over the sea.' He frowned. 'I thought it was funny that, although I could see Jack swimming out to the raft that's moored just off what we call 'Skinny Point', I couldn't see a soul. Of course, I wasn't specifically looking for Nina, because I hadn't seen her earlier. But I remember thinking, 'Oh well, on my tod again.' Then, as I came back down the path, realising that it looked very much like rain, I started to hurry. Sure enough, as I reached the beach the first drops of rain fell. I deliberately hadn't taken my watch to the beach that morning to prove to Louise I could be chilled out on holiday! But I should think I'd only been gone about twelve to fifteen minutes. Apparently I arrived back at the beach at two fifteen.'

'How d'you know that?' asked Kirsty.

'Because Jack was there and I asked him. That's another thing I'm really clear about: Jack towelling himself down in the rain and glancing at his watch. Then I asked where the others were. He told me that, as he came in from swimming, Nina had gesticulated to him from Skinny Point that she was going to find Louise and Toby to hurry them up a bit, because it looked like rain. And she'd been right — by now there was a thick drizzle. I think it was about then that Tracey and Tim turned up with their kids full of chips and ketchup, and I started to worry more about Louise and Toby; they seemed to have been gone much too long. Then at two twenty-five Nina came back from the cliffs holding Toby's hand, and he was crying enough to break his heart . . . '

At his words Kirsty felt her whole being going out to the little boy who had been the four-year-old Toby, and to his father, who was sitting here before her with an expression of such bleakness that her intended words of sympathy remained unsaid.

They were both quiet for a couple of moments. Somewhere in the background Kirsty registered a hoot of laughter from one of a group in the now crowded bar. Wanting so much to trust Mike, she studied his expression, but could find nothing other than sadness in it. He'd told her the truth, she comforted herself. It would have been easy to have said Nina was there on the beach with him all the time, wouldn't it? After all, he couldn't know that Nina had already told her differently.

'Well, where was Nina then?' Kirsty was surprised to find she'd spoken the words aloud. She licked dry lips. 'If she wasn't on the beach when you woke up — where was she?'

Mike sighed. 'She must have been poking about in the rock pools over by Skinny Point . . . And that had to be a first; she's not exactly into crabs . . . It transpired that she'd seen me wake up, then go down to the shore to look for Jack — she'd even seen me look round for my sweater — then set off up to the toilets without it. Unfortunately, she didn't remember any of this until later, after I'd been answering police questions for what seemed like hours, when all I wanted to do was get back to my son.'

'That must have been awful.'

As though to distance himself from the memory, he leaned back in his seat 'Yep, it was. Awful! Just like on the box. *Police: So, sir, you were on the beach asleep? Me: Yep. Police: From when till when, approximately, sir? Me: Don't know. One-ish till two-ish I suppose. Police: Until Jack arrived back from his swim? Me: Yes . . . No, hang on, I went up to the toilet. Police: Ah, that would account for Jack saying you weren't on the beach when he first came in from his swim. And what time would you say you arrived back from the toilet, sir? Me: About two fifteen. I asked Jack the time. Police: Any particular reason for wanting to establish the time, sir?'* He gave a grimace. 'On and on it went like that, until I thought I'd go mad. All I could think about was Toby. My poor kid with no mother, and a father banged up under suspicion of doing her in. Then, thank God, Nina remembered she was on the beach while I was sleeping, that she'd walked through the rock pools to Skinny Point to look out for Jack on the raft. She couldn't see him, you see, and although he'd stay out in the sea for ages, he'd often climb onto the raft for a break. Well, that was where he was.'

Was now the moment to tell Mike that Nina had told her differently — that Nina had told her she'd lied to the police in order to protect him? That when she'd looked back from Skinny Point he wasn't there? She decided to leave it for the moment, and went to a newer point that had raised a question. 'I thought you said you could see Jack swimming?'

'Yes, but that was when I was on the beach before I went up the cliff path.'

'And again, when you were at the top, you said you looked over the bay and could see Jack swimming. So how could he be on the raft?'

Mike leaned back in his seat and folded his arms. 'I don't know . . . Don't you start!'

'Start what?'

'Doubting my every word.'

Kirsty stared at him, aghast. This was terrible! 'I'm not, Mike ... I'm just trying to get it straight in my mind.'

Mike gave an attempt at a grin. 'Don't bother. If it's not straight in my mind, what hope have you got? Anyway, it's all ancient history now, isn't it? It's got nothing to do with the here and now. Nothing to do with us.'

Nervously, Kirsty licked her lips. Of course she believed Mike, and could see the difficulty in remembering accurately what had happened so long ago with any precision, then or now, but surely he must have wondered at Nina's sudden return of memory. 'Why on earth did it take so long for her to remember, though, that she was at Skinny Point, or whatever you call it, and she'd seen you on the beach *before* you came back from the toilet and she went off to find Louise?'

Mike spread his hands. 'She was confused. We all were. It's not every day this kind of thing happens. We were all in shock. First of all she thought that when she looked back from Skinny Point I *wasn't* there, so when she was interviewed, she'd assumed I'd stuck to the shoreline and gone up the cliffs to find Louise and Toby. That was why, when she saw me come down from the toilets alone, she'd gone to look for Louise herself. Unfortunately the police assumed much the same thing — that I'd gone after Louise — and when I'd found her, tossed her over the rocks, hared back along the top of the cliff and come back down the cliff path from the direction of the toilets in full view of Jack and Nina in order to make it look as though that was where I'd been all the time. They figured I could have done that quite easily in the time scale.'

'But what about Toby? No father would leave a four-year-old alone in a dangerous situation like that.'

'That's what I kept telling them. Thank God for Nina! OK, she remembered a bit late, but that's better than not remembering at all . . . '

Kirsty said nothing, just took a slow

sip of her drink. Something still didn't seem quite right.

'Look, Nina was in total shock; her teeth were chattering when she brought Toby back, and she looked terrible; and when we found Louise, well, she just collapsed! Tracey was trying to keep the kids calm, but Nina was in pieces. You've no idea . . . ' Mike looked away from Kirsty. 'You've no idea what we all went through, no idea at all!'

Kirsty bit her lip. What right did she have to be questioning him? Wasn't it enough that he hadn't lied to her? He'd made no excuses about the part he'd played in that far-away drama, no attempt to shirk telling her in as much painful detail as he could remember about the tragedy that had so affected him and his son. As for Nina, perhaps she'd never made it clear to Mike that she'd lied for him. Or perhaps, more likely, she *hadn't* lied for him and that was why the timing didn't quite add up. Perhaps it had been exactly as he'd said — she had been bent over the rock pools on Skinny Point and he just hadn't seen her. In which case, the only person she'd been lying to was Kirsty. And why would she do that? Kirsty asked herself.

The answer came with blinding clarity.

In order to make her think that Mike could be a wife killer?

In order to frighten her off!

'I'm sorry, Mike,' she said eventually. 'I just wanted to try and understand. I haven't quite worked out the geography, that's all, but perhaps when I'm actually on the spot I'll have a clearer grasp . . . '

She stopped as a doubtful smile gradually spread across Mike's face and he leaned across the table to take her hands. 'Actually on the spot? Does that mean you'll come? You'll really come on holiday with us . . . '

She smiled back. 'I suppose it must do,' she said.

'Hi, stranger!' A shadow fell across the table.

Kirsty looked up. 'Jo! What on earth

are you doing here?'

'That's me,' said Jo, turning her attention from their linked hands to Mike's face, with a question in her smile.

Hmm. Nothing for it; she had to make the introductions. Kirsty turned to Mike, who had got to his feet. 'Mike, this is my friend Jo — you've heard me mention her — and her boyfriend Paul.'

Jo held out a friendly hand. 'Hi, Mike. Funny, we only came in here on the spur of the moment, so — fancy meeting you two here!'

Trying to remember whether or not she'd mentioned she was coming here with Mike, and not to wonder if this was all an elaborate ruse to give Jo the opportunity to inspect Mike for suitability before Kirsty went away with him, she scrutinised her friend with suspicious eyes.

Jo flashed a pleasant smile and pulled up a chair. Paul followed suit.

'Well, now you're here . . . ' Kirsty said, looking at her friend hard. 'Join us, why not?'

It wasn't long before Paul went to fetch some drinks and Mike accompanied him to the bar in order to help carry them back to the table.

Kirsty turned to Jo. 'And what exactly *are* you doing here, Poirot?'

'I don't know what you mean, Miss Lemon,' said Jo, feigning a French accent and wide-eyed innocence. 'Paul asked where I fancied going and I said, 'The Queen's Head for a change. Kirsty came the other night and enjoyed it sooo much . . . '' She rolled her eyes. 'I quite like the look of your Mike, by the way. Lovely eyes, good bod, nice smile! And the way he looks at you — so *intense*. I could feel the smoulder at ten paces! I just had to check him out.'

'And why would that be?'

Jo gave an enigmatic smile:

'An instructor whose hair was once pink
Went out with a bloke for a drink
The silver-haired fox
Bought champagne and some chox

What happened?

Well — what do you think?'

Kirsty tried in vain to keep her face straight. 'Oh, stop looking so smug, Jo. You're such a show-off with your limericks.'

'Well, how else can I defend myself against your terrible jokes? Thought that one up in the car,' said Jo modestly. 'But he does seem nice.'

'Thanks very much, but I don't need your approval.'

Jo grinned. 'But admit it — it's nice to have it, isn't it?' Confidingly, she bent her head closer to Kirsty's. 'On a slightly more serious note, I couldn't help noticing a rather swanky red Lotus outside, and there's a sultry-looking brunette inside, filing her nails. It's parked right in the corner under the trees; I only noticed it because I must confess, I was looking for your car . . . She gave Paul the once-over and studied me for my dress size.' Jo leaned back again in her seat. 'Just watch yourself on the way home, and you'd better check on Tiger — we might have a bunny-boiler on our hands.'

Kirsty gave a weak smile. 'It might not be her,' she said shakily.

'No, but I suggest Paul and I leave at the same time you do and follow you home. I also suggest we have a nice chatty night out. I think the guys will talk footy and we can put in an odd word here and there. It was time you introduced us; I was beginning to think he had two heads or something . . . Ah, cheers, Mike!' Smilingly, she took the glass of wine Mike was holding out to her. 'I was just saying to Kirsty, the old gang keep asking after her, particularly Ed. He's *really* fond of Kirsty.'

Honestly, as though anyone would fall for that. Kirsty blushed at the obviousness of the remark.

But Mike's eyes narrowed. 'Oh?'

Perhaps not so obvious then? In spite of herself, her heart lifted. 'Don't take any notice of Jo,' she said. 'She exaggerates everything.'

Mike swallowed.

Kirsty struggled not to laugh out

loud in triumph, because at the mention of Ed, just for a second she thought she'd seen the hint of jealousy in Mike's eyes. And although, of course, she'd never do anything deliberately to cause this it was, without a doubt, satisfying to think that he cared about her enough to feel a little unsettled at the thought of an 'Ed' on the edges of her life, who also found her attractive.

By this time, as Jo had predicted, Paul was now engaging Mike in footy talk and Jo exchanged a glance with her that said, 'Told you so; a little spot of competition never hurt anyone.' Kirsty dropped her eyes, thinking that perhaps in spite of the limericks, Jo wasn't such a bad friend to have after all.

For the rest of the evening, she tried to put the idea of Nina, resolutely stalking her for possibly the rest of her life, firmly out of her mind. Nevertheless, when, after a pleasant hour or so full of friendly banter, they finally left the pub and Jo whispered to her that the red sports job was no longer there, she heaved a sigh of relief.

'I'll call you later,' she whispered to her friend as she gave her a heartfelt goodbye hug. 'Thanks for looking out for me.'

★ ★ ★

It was Saturday evening and Toby was in the utility room busy pairing up socks. Pairing up the socks and sorting the pants into Dad's pile and his own pile was a job he'd learned to do from an early age. Grandma was up the other end of the long, narrow space, putting T-shirts and school shirts and his dad's smart shirts onto hangers straight from the tumble drier — there was less ironing that way. In the background he could hear the tumble drier still operating with some of his dad's jeans inside.

It was just Grandma and him tonight, which he didn't really mind because there wasn't much on television; and when they'd finished sorting the washing they were going to have a game of

Uno, which he quite liked. Recently, Grandma had tried to teach him cribbage, but he'd said it made his brain ache, so luckily Grandma had put it away and now they stuck to draughts, dominoes, or Uno. Uno was his favourite, although of course it was better with three — but tonight Dad had gone to the pub with Kirsty.

Somehow, Toby didn't mind when Dad was out with Kirsty. He wondered if his Mum would mind and didn't think she would. He considered whether Mum, who was really no more than a pleasant but distant memory, would understand how he felt about Kirsty coming with them on the holiday. Kirsty was so much fun. So, so *not bothered* about things. She laughed easily, and didn't mind that he was there with them a lot of the time. She played with Buddy and didn't care when his black-and-white hairs stuck to her clothes. And most of all, when she was around, Dad looked happy. Not that he looked *un*happy at other times, just as though quite often his mind was on other things, but when Kirsty was close by he seemed to forget about those other things and enjoy what was happening now. Considering that Saskia wasn't there to help with things, Toby thought that was surprising. Usually when Saskia wasn't there for some reason or another, Dad would spend ages deciding what to eat and whether or not it constituted a balanced meal — whatever that was! Toby had visions of a waiter on a unicycle, balancing all the ingredients on a silver tray in the air above him. But now, if they hadn't got anything planned for dinner, they'd have fish fingers or even baked beans on toast with a poached egg on top. Toby grinned — it suited him! Once they'd even gone to the pub to eat — and on a school night! It had taken Toby some time to get over that one.

'What'll you have to drink, Toby? A pint?' Dad had said to Toby with a grin. Toby still found that difficult to believe.

'What are you grinning at?' asked Grandma, breaking into Toby's thoughts.

'Dad making a joke,' said Toby.

'Good. He should do it more often,' said Grandma, gently placing Dad's green sweater on a drying rack.

Toby stared fixedly at the green sweater.

Sweater, sweater, sweater, said a voice in his brain. Something to remember about a *sweater, sweater, sweater* . . . He'd remembered it before — but now it had gone again. That horrible strange feeling was creeping over him again.

Toby blinked hard.

Sweater, that was a funny word. Perhaps it meant you should put it on if you were sweating. No, that didn't make sense. You'd be more likely to take it off — not put it on. Sometimes Grandma called it a pullover. Now that made sense — a warm thing to pull on over other things, when you were cold. What about jumper? Something you took off before you jumped around?

'Well, if you've finished, Toby, perhaps you'd like to find the dominoes.'

'Can't we play Uno?' said Toby, glad that the funny feeling had gone away again. 'I won last time.'

'So you did,' said Grandma, stifling a yawn with a smile. 'OK, Uno it is — again!'

★ ★ ★

'Kirsty? It's Sam.'

'Oh, hello, Sam. I didn't know you had my number.'

'I asked Mum for it. I've just found out about you going to Devon with Mike and Toby. I'm so pleased.'

Kirsty shifted from one foot to the other. She was between classes and standing in the far corner of the snack bar of the sports club, where she would be taking an aqua class in five minutes. 'Well, there are others going too,' she said.

'Yes, I know but . . . There's a bit of a history.'

'Yes, I know. Mike's explained. I'm glad he did.'

'Usually Mum and I make sure one of us goes with them, just to keep an extra eye on Toby, but we thought Saskia would be with them this year and she's very capable and sensible, and we mustn't mollycoddle Tobes for ever . . . '

'Of course not,' agreed Kirsty. 'But have you spoken to Mike about this?'

'Mike's a bloke.'

'Yes, I'd noticed.'

'Bloke's don't talk about feelings. Especially not to their sisters. And the thing is, Mike thinks Toby's fine about it. But Mum and I, well, we're not so sure. There's something about Devon that unsettles him. It's as though he can't wait to go because he dimly remembers having good times there, but when he gets there, he gets the shivers for a bit . . . Saskia has always kept very close to him on these holidays.'

'Well, I'm sure the others watch him too.'

'I know, but I thought that Mike might be a bit less observant with you around . . . Oh dear, that came out all wrong, but there's no denying you're a distraction, and rightly too. It's just that without Mum or me or Saskia, I'm a little uneasy about things. You know, the ratio of adults to children?'

'I'm sure it'll be fine,' said Kirsty, thinking of the number of children she took in a swimming session. 'Children have far more sense than they're credited with, I can assure you. Anyway, I understand Nina and Jack will be there; they haven't got any children. That should bring the odds up a bit.'

'True, but Jack's a loner. Pleasant, but doesn't get too involved. Swims, sunbathes, goes to the pub, but doesn't really notice what's going on around him. And Nina . . . well, her world revolves around herself. Surely you've noticed?'

Kirsty gave a small laugh. 'Why are you all friends with her, when none of you like her very much?'

A sigh came down the phone. 'Why indeed? Long story . . . I suppose part of the trouble is, Mike met Louise through Nina.'

'Oh?'

'Yes. You couldn't be expected to

know. Louise was Nina's best friend.' Kirsty closed her eyes. She was sick of hearing what buddies Nina and Louise used to be. 'Although actually, I don't think Louise was quite so enamoured of Nina as all that. I think she was just sorry for her ... Nina can't have children, you know. Had a bit of a tough time as a kid too, by all accounts. Similar to Louise, whose mother died of cancer when she was in her teens.'

Immediately Kirsty felt sympathy towards the Louise she'd never known. 'Oh?'

'Yes, that's why she was so very close to Tobes I think. Louise's dad remarried and had another family that Louise told me she always felt she didn't quite belong to. Consequently, as teenagers, she and Nina spent a lot of time together. She couldn't just drop her, could she?'

'No, I can quite see that.'

'Anyway, apart from all that ... I'm so glad you're going to be there. I feel as though I can trust you.'

'Well, that's nice.'

'Yes, it is.'

There was silence for a moment while Kirsty wondered how to end the conversation.

'I mustn't keep you, though,' said Sam. 'You sound busy. See you soon, I hope.'

Kirsty slipped her phone back into her bag. She was unsure whether the call had been good or bad. Good in that Sam liked her — and more, trusted her enough to confide in; bad in the knowledge that Sam shared her fears that something was just not right, which added to her feeling of responsibility.

All the way through the next forty-five minutes, which constituted the aqua class, Kirsty tried to persuade herself that her fears were unfounded. Through the splashing of the skiing exercises, the feet on wall then kicking back, the jogging across the pool, the hands in the air — 'Come on ladies, let's get rid of those bingo wings', Kirsty wondered if she should do what every ounce of her intuition was screaming at her to do; tell

Mike she'd reconsidered and wouldn't be coming with them to Devon. Yes, she'd do it tonight, after the pilates class, after Toby's swimming lesson, after she'd taken him home, or possibly after they'd all had supper together. Simple!

Or, not so simple.

She'd reckoned without Toby. A Toby who was delighted to know Kirsty was coming with them on the holiday. A Toby who couldn't stop chattering about the places they could go, about the sands at Woolacombe, the village of Clovelly where no cars were allowed and the main street was so steep you had to hold on to each other in order to stay upright. That was where he'd saved Rosie once from falling over and rolling right down to the bottom. 'She wouldn't have killed herself or anything,' he'd said through a series of blinks and leg swings, 'but she would have had some nasty bumps and bruises. Tim called me a hero!'

Listening to his unrelenting enthusiasm, Kirsty realised that it was too late, far too late now, to back out.

9

'Why don't you call me Tobes?'

Kirsty looked up from her unpacking. Toby was sitting on the edge of her bed, watching her. 'I don't know. Seemed a bit of a cheek, I thought.' She took a dress — the only one she'd brought with her — and hung it up on an old wooden hanger she found in the wardrobe.

'That's a pretty dress,' said Toby, eyeing the pink, flowery, long summer dress with approval.

'I don't know if I'll get the chance to wear it,' said Kirsty doubtfully. 'If the weather doesn't cheer up I'll probably have to spoil it with a sweater on top, which wasn't really the plan.' She looked ruefully at the spattering of rain on the window pane, then back at Toby.

He'd gone as white as a sheet.

She straightened in alarm and put a

hand on his shoulder. 'What's the matter, Toby?' Toby was staring glassy-eyed in front of him. She shook him slightly. He didn't respond. 'Toby, can you hear me? What's wrong?'

He blinked. 'I'm all right,' he said, immediately attempting a smile. 'Just that sw-*sweater* is a funny word . . . I mean, does it mean you sweat if you wear one?' His colour had come back and he looked better. It was just as though a switch had been thrown.

'I don't know,' said Kirsty slowly. 'It might be.'

'I wouldn't mind, though, if you called me Tobes . . . Mum called me Tobes, and Sam and Dad both do. Not Grandma, though; she calls me Toby or 'sweetheart'.'

Kirsty shut the wardrobe door with a click. 'That's nice. Brad calls you Tobes, though, and Nina.'

Toby sighed. 'Yes, I wish she wouldn't . . . But *you* can. You can call me Tobes.'

Kirsty gave a wide smile. 'OK. Tobes

it is. Now, I expect Buddy's wondering where you are. If you can give me five minutes to freshen up, I'll come down to the kitchen in a bit and we'll see what we can find to eat.'

'We're going to Bideford for fish and chips,' said Toby. 'Dad promised. He said we owed you fish and chips.'

'Yummy.' Exaggeratedly, Kirsty rolled her eyes. 'OK, then. I'll be down shortly.'

When Toby had gone, she looked after him thoughtfully for a moment. Was that an example of the kind of behaviour Sam was so worried about? What had she said: that once he got there, Devon gave Toby the shivers? Was it another frozen moment, like the one on the diving board? A moment goodness knew what had triggered, turning Toby into a small statue of fear, before he blinked and returned to normality. Could it be a medical matter? Something a doctor should know about?

Then she shook herself. Who was she to start panicking, and suggesting doctors? He'd lost concentration for a moment, that was all. If he needed medical attention, Mike would be the first to know and act upon it. She'd watch him, though, and if there were another incident like the one she'd just witnessed she'd have to bring it to Mike's attention, whether he thought she was interfering or not.

Kirsty frowned and, with a small shrug of her shoulders, turned to stare out at the scudding clouds. She shivered as another burst of rain blew against the window. Her room was on the top floor and looked over the rooftops towards the sea which, even from here, appeared cold and grey. It felt more like Yorkshire than Devon and Mike, in the couple of weeks leading up to the trip, had been more like Heathcliff than the relaxed holiday-ish Mike she'd hoped for. In all fairness, though, he'd been terribly busy trying to make sure that the kitchen he was currently building would carry on successfully in his absence, and he still had to share the school run with Anne. All of which didn't leave much time.

She sighed. Despite the fact that she'd managed to get Mike into her flat on two occasions, those times had been fleeting, because either Toby was with him or he'd come only in order to pick her up and go on elsewhere. He'd admired the cosy flat, fondled Tiger's ears, and remarked upon the view, but looked uncomfortable throughout.

Resolutely, she turned from the window. Now that the holiday had started, however, surely things would be different. Certainly they should be able to snatch some time, just the two of them — alone — and she would be able to decide if there was to be any future for them together.

For Kirsty determined that this holiday was to be the decider: the make-or-break of the relationship. That was the reason she had brought her own car. She'd made the excuse that her car was more able to negotiate the narrow, winding Devon lanes than Mike's larger, heavier vehicle. But really, she acknowledged to herself now, it was because if she wanted to, she could beat a hasty retreat. Although the friendly Tracey and family were due to turn up at any moment, Jack and Nina would be arriving tomorrow; and if Nina was going to be a constant on the scene, Kirsty wasn't sure how long she would stay the course. Thank goodness Nina and Jack had their own cottage. If they hadn't, Kirsty had the feeling she would have declined the invitation in the first place.

At the sound of Mike's voice from downstairs, followed by his low laugh, her face broke into a smile. She imagined him standing there, ruefully pulling at his ear as he contemplated the terrible weather. Her smile broadened. It was up to her to reassure him the rain didn't matter a jot. Pulling a wry face at herself in the mirror, she applied some fresh lip gloss, then straightened her shoulders. Mike and Toby, two of her very favourite people, were downstairs waiting. Why should she care about Nina? And what difference would a bit of bad weather make? There was the whole holiday before them and she was about to make the most of it.

Humming a snatch of 'Singing in the Rain', she executed a smart tap step before running down the stairs.

★   ★   ★

Thankfully, the next morning dawned bright and sunny. After enjoying a prolonged breakfast round the large kitchen table, the children and an excitable Buddy were all in the garden playing on the climbing frame which, it appeared, was far superior to the one they had at home. It was higher and had a pulley with a basket on it. This provided them with the ability to lift stones and slates, of which there were plenty, up to the top of the tower for the building of battlements. It was only when Rosie was sent in with a request for boiling water to pour on the heads of the attacking army, that a halt was called to that particular game, and Kirsty started clearing the breakfast dishes away.

Leaving Kirsty's small car on the drive, which was large enough to take several vehicles, they all piled into the two larger cars and drove to the nearest beach, where they parked before exploring the shoreline. There were long stretches of sand interceded with cliffs which fell away to the sea in long steep slopes, creating lots of intriguing rock pools. Distracted by the fascinating creatures lurking in the trapped shallows, the children lagged behind along with Tim and Mike, and Kirsty found herself walking ahead with Tracey. Buddy bounded gleefully between the two groups, barking at the sea gulls, and grinning all over his sandy face.

'We weren't sure you'd come,' said Tracey. 'Mike was a nervous wreck waiting for you to make up your mind.'

'Really?' Kirsty laughed. 'Well, I wasn't sure at first, but . . . well, here I am.'

'It's good,' went on Tracey. 'It's really good to see that at last Mike's moving on.'

Kirsty could think of no reply.

Negotiating the odd finger of dark grey rocks that formed one of the many natural piers along the coastline, Kirsty began to see how caves and bays could remain hidden from the top of the cliffs or boats at sea. 'Beautiful here, isn't it?' she said, pausing a moment to shade her eyes and look further along the coast. She lifted her arm and pointed. 'Is that the direction of the beach where Louise fell?'

'I wondered whether you'd ask that . . . No, it's all right, it's only natural that you're curious . . . Yes, Louise's beach — she discovered it, so we call it that — is to the north of here, further along the coast. The coast road isn't very coastal just here, you see; too many rocks and inlets, so it has to go quite far inland . . . Louise's beach is a lovely little hidden bay only a bit further on from a larger, more commercial one.

You can reach it by an old narrow coastal road with no room for passing traffic, but there's a longish climb down so not too many people use it, or even know of its existence. But anyway, nowadays we go south of here, more Woolacombe or Braunton way. The sands are lovely there.' She looked away for a moment, but not before Kirsty had glimpsed the sadness in her eyes. 'No, we don't go to Louise's beach so much anymore . . . Well, never, really.'

'I suppose not.'

Tracey tucked a piece of auburn hair behind her ear. 'I think Mike was right to keep coming back, though. It's a sort of continuity with happier times. You can't wipe out the whole of the past, even if you do have to move on.'

Kirsty glanced sideways. Tracey's face was calm and impassive again. 'You don't think it's too unsettling for Toby, then?' she asked her.

'Oh, Tobes just tends to get on with things. Luckily, he doesn't remember anything about the accident. He is a bit sensitive sometimes, but I put that down to him being an only child. Mainly, he's just a normal eight-year-old and of course, being with our kids helps. They get on very well together — always have done.'

'Yes, well, you have a lovely family; they do you credit,' said Kirsty. 'They must have been upset too, especially the older ones.'

'We explained it as best we could at the time, and they're very careful on any cliffs now . . . But you can't keep children away from danger for ever; they're fascinated by it. All you can do is try to make them understand it and hold their hands while they test the waters.'

Kirsty hesitated. Should she tell Tracey about Toby — his unexpected freezing on the diving board, his sudden strangeness at the word 'sweater'? Watching Tracey's expression closely, she haltingly began telling her about what had happened at the swimming pool. Tracey listened carefully without interrupting.

'You told Mike about it afterwards?'

she asked when Kirsty had finished.

Kirsty nodded. 'Yes, and he clarified that Toby could remember nothing of the accident . . . But then yesterday, a similar thing happened.' She went on to explain, but even as she was doing so she realised how much it sounded as though she was over-reacting.

But Tracey had stopped walking. 'Now that *is* strange,' she said.

Kirsty opened her mouth to ask why, when there was a sudden shout from close behind them — and when she swivelled round she saw Toby running towards them, holding up a bucket where he had obviously deposited something interesting, ready for inspection.

They turned together and made their way back to the rock pools.

The day passed easily enough. They'd brought some rugs to sit on, and sandwiches and drinks, which they ate sitting together on a convenient flat rock. The sun was warm and the wind had dropped. Soon there was only the murmuring of the sea and the cries of the seagulls to be heard. Tracey lay back on her rug and Tim sat next to her, hugging his knees and keeping a watchful eye on the children. The water was creeping in, but Kirsty was told that the best time for the children to venture in was when it covered the first stretch of sand. 'Otherwise there are stubbed toes and lots of whinging and whining,' said Tim.

Mike got to his feet. 'I'm for a walk up the beach,' he said. 'Are you coming, Kirsty?' He put out a hand in order to haul her to her feet, and it seemed the most natural thing in the world to take it and walk along the sand next to him with her hand in his.

They walked in silence until they were way out of the others' hearing.

'I want to apologise,' he said suddenly.

'What for?'

'I feel as though I've neglected you the last couple of weeks.'

'Well, you've had a lot on your plate.'

'That's no excuse. I wanted everything to be right and when I get harassed, I go quiet. I don't mean to . . . I'm sorry.'

He gave a sigh. 'I suppose you think I'm a moody devil.'

'I wouldn't say moody . . . Well, one mood really.'

Mike looked anxious. 'And what's that?'

The corners of Kirsty's lips curved. 'Controlled.'

He thought for a moment. 'OK . . . I'd agree. But not controlling. Controlled, yes. Have to be, really.'

'Why?'

'Because . . . because I have responsibilities. Double responsibilities where Toby's concerned.'

'Ever heard the expression 'all work and no play'?'

'Easy for you to say.'

Kirsty bent down and retrieved a shell. 'Yeah, maybe . . . ' She contemplated the shell for a moment before tossing it back on the sand. Then, spontaneously, she turned towards him. 'Oh, don't you ever feel like running, shouting, screaming? Just for the fun of it.'

Mike looked at her, his eyes clear and

the colour of the sea. He gave a small apologetic grin. 'Once upon a time . . . Then I grew up.'

Facing him now, Kirsty took his hands and looked deep into his eyes. Darn it. There was something so vulnerable about him, yet so potently attractive. Her definitely out-of-control heart was beating wildly. 'Mike,' she started and leaned closer. Then she looked over his shoulder to where the tiny shapes of Tracey and Tim sat, the four children with their individual bent postures no more than stick figures in the distance. She gave an awkward laugh and pulled back. 'OK, let's just see if you *can* run,' she said. 'I'll race you up to that next outcrop of rocks.'

She started off fast, glancing over her shoulder with a grin after she'd covered the first few yards. Despite his surprise, Mike was rapidly catching up. She put on another spurt, but he was suddenly level and about to pass her.

Clutching her ankle, she fell to her knees with a small scream. Mike slowed, turned and came back. 'Are you all right? Here, let me . . . '

But Kirsty was on her feet again and off like a bullet. No looking back this time. Exhilaration pumped through her veins, urging her on even though she was getting short of breath. She loved to run. Just the joy of running was enough on its own, but knowing that Mike was behind her made her enjoyment all the more keen.

Finally, with Mike only a nose behind her, she reached the rocks and, with a triumphant whoop, bent over with her hands on her knees in an effort to recover her breath. 'Beat you,' she panted.

'Only because a) you cheated and b) I let you,' Mike managed to get out between his own gasps.

Kirsty sank down on the nearest rock. 'Liar. You're just as done in as I am.'

Mike sank down next to her. 'You're a mad, bad lady, d'you know that?'

Squinting against the sun, she looked up at him. 'How bad?'

The sun was blotted out as he

reached over her. 'This bad,' he said cupping her chin in his hand, his mouth finding hers.

★   ★   ★

Toby felt happy.

He'd caught the biggest crab of them all. He'd taught a reluctant-at-first Buddy that the water was a good place to be. When the sea was close enough, they'd gone in and done pretend diving through the waves, and Brad had told him his swimming was pretty cool. Dad and Kirsty had come back from their walk looking flushed and happy, and they were all going to have hamburgers and baked beans for supper!

Admittedly, he'd felt a bit funny once or twice. Like when Rosie had suddenly said to look up at the cliffs because she thought she could see a dog stuck. But it hadn't been a dog, just a black plastic bag, and Toby had managed to lower his eyes slowly from the cliffs so that they didn't look quite so . . . He didn't want to think about the word 'frightening'. So he didn't; he played with Rosie instead. They spelled out her name in the sand and then they went to look for more limpets and red, green, and orange anemones in the rock pools. He didn't even mind when bossy Jenny came along and started to explain what a periwinkle was. As if he didn't know already!

Anyway, that had been that, and they'd collected up their things and gone back to the car, and Dad had ruffled Brad's hair and asked if he wanted to ride with them. When he'd said yes, Dad had said, 'Hamburgers and baked beans for supper then, eh?'

Could life get much better? Toby didn't think so.

★　★　★

The hamburgers and baked beans had gone down well. When they were done with eating, Tracey and Tim disappeared into one of the sitting rooms along with all the children, and Mike volunteered to make coffee. Quietly, Kirsty followed him into the kitchen.

He looked round. 'Hiya!' he said, grinning in that special way that made his eyes twinkle. She watched as he filled the percolator and set out four cups.

'You've done this before,' said Kirsty, sitting down at the table and wishing she didn't find him quite so attractive. His hair had gone more silver, his tan had deepened, and his mouth . . . well, his mouth always looked so kissable. It was a struggle for her to keep her mind on anything when he was sitting opposite her with a mouth like that!

'I'll take theirs through and we'll have ours outside, shall we?'

'Great. Love to.' Kirsty got to her feet again and went outside to put cushions on the garden bench. 'This is nice,' she said two minutes later, when Mike was sitting beside her with his hand holding hers.

'Yes, and it's only the first day. We've got all week.'

They sat in silence for a while, the soft Devon air folding round them as the sun moved lower in the sky. 'It's peaceful here, isn't it?' Kirsty said.

'Yes,' answered Mike. 'That's one of the reasons I love it so much. Different pace of life, more gentle, more relaxed.' He looked at her in sudden alarm. 'I hope you won't find it boring,' he said as though it had only just occurred to him. 'There's not much night life here. The most exciting entertainment is a pub quiz now and then, although I'm hoping that Tracey and Tim will look after the kids a couple of nights so we can go to a decent restaurant, and vice-versa of course.'

'Sounds good.'

'I hope so, Kirsty. I really hope so.' Suddenly, as though unable to help himself, he leaned forward and kissed her. It was a slow, gentle kiss, unlike the earlier feverish kisses they had snatched on the beach. Those had been kisses that could have easily turned to a passion difficult to turn off.

'I wish,' he started, staring into her eyes. 'I wish . . . '

Kirsty put her fingers on his lips. 'Don't wish,' she said. 'It's beautiful here. Let's not spoil the moment. We have plenty of time.'

They sipped their coffee slowly, just as though they were a long-established couple who didn't feel the need for talking. There was the subdued sound of the television from inside, the occasional murmur of voices, and then the rumble of Tim's laughter.

Eventually, Mike looked at his watch. 'We'll have to get those kids to bed in a minute,' he said, 'or they'll be grumpy all day tomorrow . . . Anyway, it's getting a bit cooler now. Shall I bring you a sweater if you want to stay out here?'

At the word 'sweater' Kirsty stiffened, suddenly remembering that on the beach earlier, Tracey had been going to tell her something triggered by the word. 'No,' she said to Mike. 'Don't worry. I'll come in and tidy the kitchen while you get Toby sorted out.'

'Tim and I will see to the kids,' said Mike when they got inside.

Tracey, who was already half-asleep on the sofa, yawned widely. 'Lovely,' she said. 'Lovely.'

After the children — without too much complaint — had dragged themselves up the stairs, followed by the two men, Kirsty sat down next to Tracey on the sofa. 'Back to what we were saying earlier,' she started.

Tracey looked at her blankly.

'You said it was odd when I told you about Toby's reaction to the word 'sweater'.'

'Oh yes.' Tracey was more alert now. 'Yes, it did just strike me as being strange. There was such a hoo-ha over Mike's sweater, you know — at the time of the accident. He said he was looking for it on the beach, you see, because it had suddenly become cold.'

Kirsty nodded, somehow knowing that she wasn't going to like what was coming next.

'Well,' said Tracey, 'Mike's sweater

was found under Louise's body.'

It was like a kick in the teeth. 'Oh!'

'But, although the police did go on about it at first, it was all right in the end, because Nina said that she'd seen Louise take it with her when she'd taken Toby for his walk . . . So the police were happy with that — eventually.'

A cold feeling was making its way up Kirsty's spine. 'And what did Mike say?'

'Mike couldn't remember. Mike was in shock. If you'd told him the moon was made of cheese he'd have believed it. But there were lots of questions asked about that sweater. Tim and I couldn't even remember what colour it was, and anyway we'd already left with the kids before Louise went up the cliffs.'

'What about Jack?'

'Jack couldn't say for certain, either.'

'Well then that seems a reasonable explanation to me.' Kirsty wasn't sure who she was trying to convince. She thought it might be herself. 'Louise took the sweater — must have done . . . I suppose Toby took in more than you all think, and odd things that worried him are coming back?'

Tracey stretched and yawned again. 'I expect so,' she said. 'Strange, though, after all this time.'

Strange, and disturbing. How could she face Mike now? There was no way she could confront him in front of Tracey and Tim. But, just as Tim and Mike returned downstairs, there was the sound of a car drawing up outside.

Tracey pulled a face. 'Oh crikey,' she said. 'That'll be Jack and Nina, and here I was hoping for an early night.'

The back door opened. 'Hiya!' Nina, as usual, looked as though she'd stepped out of the pages of *Vogue*, and Jack came in behind her carrying a bottle of champagne.

Kirsty smiled hello and, still with all sorts of unanswered questions churning around in her brain, tried to fade into the background as Mike appeared from upstairs and smilingly greeted the newcomers. After Mike had introduced Jack to Kirsty, she picked up her bag from where she'd parked it on the kitchen windowsill, and was about to murmur that she had some calls she must make, when Nina sauntered over.

'I see you've brought your pumpkin with you,' she said, eyeing Kirsty's orange handbag with sardonic amusement.

'Yes, but don't worry, I've left my cat and my collapsible broomstick at home,' replied Kirsty with an edge to her voice, because for once, she wasn't in the mood for jokes.

'Oh we're not staying,' said Nina. 'Just wanted to let you know we've arrived safely and to leave my car here. Only room for Jack's car in our pocket-handkerchief-sized spot, so I'll leave mine here, if that's OK, Mike?'

'Of course,' said Mike.

Glasses of bubbly were passed round, a toast made to happy holidays, and a few more words were exchanged. Tim and Jack had a conversation about fishing and flood warnings and too much rain or not enough; Nina stood very close to Mike and spoke in a low voice about something she obviously didn't want Kirsty to hear. Eventually, Kirsty had had enough, and with a murmured 'night', sidled out of the kitchen and went up to her room. She didn't come down again until she heard Jack's car start.

When she did so, she found that Tim and Tracey were going up to bed.

'Where did you get to?' asked Mike after good nights had been said.

'I felt somewhat surplus to requirements,' said Kirsty, aware that, for maybe the first time in her life, she felt jealous.

Mike looked puzzled.

Suddenly her patience snapped. 'Oh, grow up Mike. Nina's all over you. Whenever she's in your vicinity she's all over you like a rash.' Oh well, she'd said it now! 'You must have noticed!' she added for good measure.

Mike looked uncomfortable and pulled his ear. 'She's had some problems . . . I owe her.'

Kirsty's heart sank. 'What kind of problems, and what do you owe her, exactly?'

'It's hard to explain.'

'Try.'

Mike looked across at her. 'She was Louise's best friend,' he started.

'So everyone keeps telling me.'

'She was almost as cut up as I was.'

Kirsty nodded.

'After it — the accident — happened, we . . . we talked to each other a lot . . . Look, I'm not proud of this . . . '

'You're going to tell me that one thing led to another, right?'

'No! But, very nearly. I was being selfish, just talking about Louise, on and on. As though somehow it would help. And suddenly she — well, she . . . '

'Came on to you?'

'Well, yes. And I was surprised, I suppose.'

'And lonely?'

270

'Certainly that. But actually, believe it or not, I realised I didn't even like her and I was horrified.'

'How horrified?'

'Enough to stop . . . Enough to feel sorry for her.'

There was a long silence.

'Mike?'

Mike looked up. 'Yes?'

'Why didn't you tell me about the sweater?'

'The sweater?' he repeated slowly.

'Yes, *your* sweater. The one that was found under Louise's body.'

Mike rubbed his forehead. 'I was going to. I was about to when we were at the pub . . . Honestly, I was about to. If you remember, your friend Jo turned up and the moment passed. Then it sort of went out of my mind.'

'OK. So tell me now.'

'It's nothing, really. It's just that I was so sure I'd had it on the beach, so sure that Louise went off without it; but then, thankfully, Nina remembered that Louise had it with her. You see, I do

271

owe Nina — big time. She got me off the hook. It could have been so much worse than it was.'

Gently, Kirsty shook her head. 'If all she did was to tell the truth — how can you *owe* her?'

Mike's eyes met hers for a long moment. 'If? What d'you mean — if?'

'Well, if it *was* the truth, it doesn't pan out, does it?'

Mikes face closed. 'Doesn't it?' He turned his back to her and put the coffee cups in the dishwasher. 'You seem to have an unhealthy preoccupation with my past.'

'Well, if I do, it's because *your* past is part of *my* present and it contains too much unfinished business!' This time the silence seemed interminable. Kirsty found herself blinking back some tears. 'Oh, Mike. Talk to me!'

Without looking at her, Mike continued to stack the dishes. 'I've tried it. You didn't seem to be listening. I've told you all I remember. What more can I do?'

After watching his rigid back for a few more moments, Kirsty sighed. 'Good night, then,' she said as she left the room.

But Mike didn't answer.

10

After a dreadful night, Kirsty woke to the sound of children's television on at high volume. Groaning, she looked at her watch. Nine thirty! Goodness, she rarely slept so late. Miserably, she turned onto her side and tried to be positive about what the day might bring. Well, one thing was for sure — she couldn't stay here in bed for much longer, or it would appear that she was sulking. But on the other hand, the thought of breezing into the kitchen wishing everyone a 'good morning' when it was patently obvious, to her at least, that it was anything but, was not an attractive alternative.

She peered out of the window. Not too bad. Even if it wasn't going to be a scorcher, at least the sky was bluish and the sun was trying its best to escape from behind a cloud.

After a speedy shower, she pulled on some jeans and a T-shirt, picked up her orange bag and a fleece to match, and made her way slowly down the stairs. As she passed the television room she peeked in to see a row of pyjama-clad children sitting on the carpet, mesmerised by a cartoon. Even Jenny the super-cool kid sat entranced by what was on the screen. Kirsty tiptoed on past and through to the kitchen which, thankfully, was empty. She tested the kettle with her hand. It was warm, and there was a large teapot three quarters full of tea on the surface next to it. She heard the boiler fire up again and guessed there were a few showers going on in other parts of the house.

Good. She took a pen from her bag and scrawled a note. *Gone out for a drive in order to get my bearings. Be a couple of hours but don't wait for me, I'll be fine. Kirsty.*

She stuck the note on the window sill where someone was bound to find it, drank a glass of orange and took a banana from the fruit bowl, then headed for the back door.

The key was in the lock. She turned it.

'Where are you going?'

Kirsty leapt as though she'd been shot. 'Oh, it's you, Toby. You made me jump.'

'Where are you going?' repeated a spiky-haired, sleepy-eyed Toby doggedly.

'Just for a bit of a recce.'

'Can I come with you?'

Kirsty gave a half-laugh. 'You're busy, aren't you? And you're only half-dressed.'

'I can be quick.'

Kirsty sighed. 'No, Toby, not this time. You stay and have your breakfast with your dad.'

'He wouldn't mind. You know he wouldn't.'

'Sorry, Tobes. Not this time. There's something I want to see for myself, by myself. It's a geography thing.'

Toby blinked hard. 'Oh,' he said.

'I'll see you later. Promise.'

She glanced across at Nina's sleek

red jobby. Loads of power under that bonnet. She started her own engine and let out the clutch. OK. So, she knew the direction of Louise's beach; all she had to do was keep going along the coastal road until she reached a left turn-off that looked as though it went nowhere, then follow it, keeping a sharp lookout for a pull-off half-hidden from the road, with an old toilet shack and room for a few cars to park. Simple!

As she drove, she recognised the beach they'd visited yesterday and thought she spotted the steep cliff that rose in the distance and hid the two bays from view. She kept driving. Quite why she wanted to see the scene of the accident, she wasn't sure; only that until she did, she'd never quite understand the sequence of events that had resulted in such a bizarre finale.

She'd hoped that maybe it was something she and Mike would have been able to do together; but after last night, that was out of the question. Perhaps the most sensible course of action would be to admit defeat. Go home to Christchurch right now, before she could become any further entangled in the emotional net that was closing round her. Because, after a night's soul-searching, she knew full well where her heart was leading her; knew that she was falling quite desperately in love with Mike. But in the small hours, she'd admitted to herself that she would never be content to let the past lie. She needed to know that not only she, but Mike as well — and yes, even Toby — were at peace with the past, whatever that past was. It felt to her as though all of them were in limbo-land. And limbo-land wasn't a comfortable place to be.

What was that? Spotting an almost imperceptible fork in the road ahead, she slowed down to first gear and carefully inched the car along it. Actually, after the first bumpy hundred yards, when all she could see was rough grass and beyond it the horizon of the sea, the road became smoother and she was aware of climbing steadily towards some kind of summit.

Two minutes later she was there. It was exactly as Mike had described it. She decided to give the toilet building a miss, but she stood looking for a long time at the view from the edge of the car park. She could see the cliffs rising steeply to the right of the secluded beach beneath her.

After pocketing her phone, she locked her bag in the boot. Her lovely orange bag. Although the possibility of it being stolen was remote, she would be sad to lose it, whether it resembled a pumpkin or not!

Her canvas shoes had good gripping soles and, without thinking too much further about it, she started towards the cliff path.

* * *

Moodily, Toby used his spoon to divide his cereal into two cliffs, with a river of milk running through the centre. A slice of banana represented a boat on Milk

River, and a sultana chopped in half made two satisfactory oars. Opposite him Rosie tried to copy his work of art, but without the same success. Well, she was a girl and only just seven; what could you expect?

'Kirsty having a late one?' Tracey asked Dad, who had come into the kitchen looking rumpled and as though he'd hardly slept.

Dad grunted.

Toby opened his mouth to say that she'd gone for a drive, but before he could, Dad gave him a look and told him to stop playing with his cereal and start eating it like a normal human being. So Toby did just that.

Grown-ups. There was just no understanding them.

★   ★   ★

Kirsty stood facing the sea. Her back was to the cliffs and the pathway that Louise and Toby must have taken up to the tall steep cliff walk, to her right.

280

Closer to her, Skinny Point was also to her right, stretching out into the sea. Moored near the end was the raft that Jack had swum to.

She frowned and looked to her left. The rocks there formed a gentler slope to the water's edge and she could see it was quite possible to walk, as Tracey and Tim and their children had done, through the rock pools and round to the other bay, which was out of sight.

So where were the others on that ill-fated day? Louise and Toby up on the cliff walk, Jack in the water swimming towards the raft, Mike asleep on the beach behind where she now stood, and Nina out on Skinny Point.

But Mike hadn't seen her there when he woke up. And at first, Nina had told the police that she hadn't seen him on the beach either.

Now why would she do that?

Kirsty clapped her hands to her head. 'Idiot!' she said aloud.

Of course, in Nina's first interview with the police she would have had no idea what they thought, or even what Mike had told them, so she told them what she thought they wanted to hear — that she was on Skinny Point watching Jack, who was swimming; and, when pressed, that when she'd looked back at the beach — *because she knew that at some stage Mike had gone up to the toilets* — Mike wasn't there. She hadn't thought any further than that. But afterwards, when it dawned on her that the police were giving Mike a hard time, she remembered what Mike had said earlier about waking up on the beach feeling cold, looking round for his sweater, walking to the sea, spotting Jack, then deciding to go on up to the toilets. When she'd realised Mike was in trouble because he had no alibi, she'd changed her story accordingly.

So, if she really *hadn't* seen Mike, *why hadn't she?*

Either he'd followed Louise up the cliff path and hadn't spotted Nina out on Skinny Point, or she hadn't seen him because although *he* was there on the beach just as he said — *she wasn't on Skinny Point.* So, if she was lying, was it just to protect Mike? Because if she really hadn't seen Mike on the beach, and he was adamant he was there, well, *where was she?* She'd said she was on the beach, because that was where everyone expected her to be. Because Jack had seen her there on Skinny Point as he came in from his swim. But earlier, when Mike had been looking over from the toilets area, Jack had been swimming, not lying on the raft as she had stated.

Maybe she hadn't lied just in order to save Mike, but also in order to give herself an alibi!

Then, there was the mystery of the sweater. Mike had been so convinced that Louise *hadn't* taken his sweater. So suppose he was right — how had his sweater ended up under the body of Louise? Kirsty sucked in her breath. There was only one answer she could think of.

An uncomfortable feeling on the

back of her neck suddenly caused her to shiver and swivel round.

'Well, well, well, fancy meeting you here!'

Less than two feet away stood Nina, who was staring at her with the eyes of a cat.

★ ★ ★

Dad was pouring out a mug of tea. He'd chosen the thin china mug that had flowers on it. He'd taken it from the back of the cupboard, given it a good wash, carefully measured out the milk, and was really making a business of it. Strange, Toby had never known him take so much trouble over a mug of tea.

As though he felt Toby's eyes on him, Dad said without even looking up, 'Toby, I want you fully dressed by the time I come back, right?' And, without waiting for an answer, he'd left the kitchen carrying the mug.

Toby shrugged as he went to comply;

Dad was definitely in a weird mood today.

Less than two minutes later Toby was sitting in the corner of the kitchen trying to put on his socks, which suddenly seemed much too small, when Dad came in again still carrying the flowery mug.

'Anyone seen Kirsty?' he asked, looking slightly anxious.

'She's gone out,' said Toby, who'd managed one sock but was still struggling with the other.

'Well, you might have told me before I took her the tea.'

'Well, I didn't know it was for her,' said Toby indignantly. 'Anyway, she said something about geography and she wanted to go on her own.'

Dad pulled at his ear and looked thoughtful.

'Here, she left a note.' Tracey picked up a folded piece of paper from the windowsill.

'Hmm,' said Dad after reading it. 'I'll just go and see if her car's missing.'

Toby sat where he was but noticed Tim raise his eyebrows in Tracey's direction, and Tracey spread her hands in a 'don't ask me' gesture, back.

'Nina's car's gone too,' said Dad, coming back. 'When you're in this kitchen at the back, you can't hear a thing!'

'Well, we know where Nina's gone,' said Tracey.

'Where's that?' asked Dad sharply.

Toby saw another exchanged glance between Tim and Tracey.

'Where she always goes on the first morning she has in Devon. She goes to Louise's beach, and picks some flowers to throw over the cliff.'

'Oh,' said Dad. 'I didn't know that.'

Tracey shrugged.

Toby felt sick and very strange. *Throw over the cliff*. A picture came into his mind: his mum standing with her back to the sky, shouting something. She was angry. Seagulls were wheeling around in all directions. And Nina, he was sure Nina was there.

'What's the matter, Toby? What's the matter, Toby? *Toby, what's the matter?*'

'Nothing,' said Toby very fast, because Dad was staring at him with concern. Out of the corner of his eye, Toby saw Tim and Tracey leave the room.

'Come on, mate,' said Dad. 'Let's get ourselves going, eh? Perhaps you haven't had enough to eat. You didn't have much cereal; how about a banana? You like those.'

'She took a banana,' said Toby. 'Kirsty. I mean. She took a banana . . . Dad, I really think we should find her. I really do. I don't want her to fall off the cliff.'

'Toby, what are you talking about? Kirsty's not going to fall off any cliff.'

Toby heard his voice rise a notch. 'You don't know. You can't know that. People have accidents all the time, you said so. You know they do . . . I want to find Kirsty. I think we should go *now*.'

'Don't get upset, Toby. Nothing like that will happen again . . . '

'Dad, I don't want there to be another fight.'

287

Dad looked puzzled. 'What d'you mean, another fight?'

'It doesn't matter. I think Kirsty's gone to Mum's beach. I don't think Nina likes her very much. I don't want there to be another accident.' Toby held his breath. 'Please, Dad, can we go there? It's important. Please!'

Dad looked at Toby for a long time. Then he straightened. 'Toby,' he said. 'Get in the car.'

* * *

'I come here every time I come to Devon,' said Nina. 'She was my best friend, you see. Oh, long before Mike came on the scene. *My* scene.'

They were walking along the beach towards the cliffs where Louise had met her death. A bunch of wildflowers were in Nina's hand.

'Mike was mine, before Louise. Yes, *I* introduced them. I remember being nervous that they wouldn't get on. My best friend and the man I loved! Ironic,

288

that . . . ' She laughed her metallic laugh. 'Within a month Mike was telling me that he and Louise were in love and that it was all over between us.'

As they passed Skinny Point, Kirsty looked at Nina's side view — the almost perfect profile; the dark, beautifully tended hair; and the long, supple limbs encased in the best casual clothing that money could buy — and found that she was feeling sorry for her.

'I put a brave face on it — didn't have a choice, really . . . ' went on Nina. 'Anyway, then I met Jack, who was fun, good-looking and loaded. So . . . ' She shrugged. 'But — the friendship continued.'

Kirsty could think of nothing to say.

Nina turned towards her with a bright smile. 'I can show you where it happened, if you like. Just so you have it clear in your mind.' Kirsty nodded, and followed as Nina began the ascent. 'It's not that steep,' Nina said over her shoulder. 'And certainly not dangerous, so long as you stay on the path. When we get to the top, you have to look out for the gullies though. That's what they think happened to Louise — that she tripped and fell down a gully.'

'Right,' said Kirsty.

It must have taken ten minutes to reach the top, where the rocks were still rugged, but the path had evened out into rough grass. They walked a little further, with Nina pointing out the deep crevasses in the rocks. 'Fantastic view,' she said stepping off the path. 'Look, you can see for miles right across the bay.'

'So you can,' agreed Kirsty, hanging back somewhat. 'I won't come too close; I'm a bit nervous of heights,' she lied.

'Well, this is where it happened,' said Nina, pointing downwards. 'Louise was found just down there.'

'Right,' said Kirsty, eyeing the flowers. 'Well, you'll want some time alone. I'll give you some space.'

'I told you,' said Toby when they drew up next to Nina's Lotus and Kirsty's more modest vehicle.

Dad looked grim. 'You'd better come with me, Toby. I can't leave you here on your own, but listen: keep out of it! When we catch up with them I'll deal with it. OK? I'm sure everything's fine, but it's grown-up stuff, so you need to be grown up too, and do what I tell you.'

Toby stared at his dad. 'Come on,' he said, starting towards the cliff path. 'We need to hurry.'

'No,' said Dad. 'Look, we can see they're not on the beach. They must have already climbed to the cliff. We'll go along the top and meet up with them. Now there's no real path, so you'll have to follow me.'

But Toby was already out of the car and running. There was a voice in his head telling him to hurry. If he hurried, he might not be too late.

* * *

The blow, when it came, took Kirsty off balance and she landed on her knees, doubled in two, every breath expelled from her lungs.

'That's for poking your nose where it doesn't belong,' said Nina triumphantly.

Fighting for breath, Kirsty stayed still with her head lowered. She knew that the edge of a crevasse was uncomfortably close. A pair of neat ankles, fashionably clad in ballet pumps, were a foot away from her. She gave an exaggerated intake of air — she hadn't learned karate for nothing. Suddenly her hands shot out and she grasped Nina's ankles and pulled hard. With a surprised yelp, Nina fell backwards onto the dried verge.

'And *that*'s for Louise and for making Mike and Toby miserable,' said Kirsty, her breath coming in short jerky gasps.

Her eyes narrowing to slits, Nina struggled to sit up.

Easily, Kirsty pushed her back down

again — hard. 'And that's for taking the mickey out of my bag, for trying to make me believe Mike was a killer and also for being a killer yourself . . . Because that's what you are, isn't it?'

Wrapping her arms around herself, Nina turned her face away. 'It was an accident,' she said quietly. 'It wasn't like that at all.'

'Well how was it, then? Just how exactly did Louise end up at the bottom of a cliff when only you and she were here?'

'I know,' said a small voice from behind her. 'I know what happened.'

Kirsty turned her head. 'Toby! Mike! What are you doing here?'

Toby was shaking. 'I t-t-told my Dad. I didn't like you being on your own with her.'

'Stay back, Toby — don't come any closer!'

'It's all right, my dad's here this time!'

Mike looked frantic. Toby looked pale. Pale but determined. 'It came back to me,' he said. 'I suddenly knew why I never liked Nina. She was up here that day . . . '

'What the hell's been going on?' It was Mike. 'What's wrong with Nina?'

'Guilty conscience, I should think . . . You can sit up now, Nina, but any funny stuff and I'll lay you out cold.' Kirsty looked towards Toby, who had that glassy-eyed look again. 'Toby wants to tell us something . . . I think we should listen.'

Toby took a shuddering breath. 'We were on our way back to the beach. We'd been collecting shells and bits of coloured rock. Mum said she wished she'd brought a s-s-sweater.' A flicker of pain passed across his face. 'I was a bit behind her, further up than this, when she said, 'Oh no, it's Nina.' I think she was as fed up with her as I was . . . Then they started arguing . . . I don't really know what about, because it was raining a bit and the path was slippery, so I was watching where my feet went. Mum told me to get behind her. Nina was in front, but I could hear their voices were cross. Then Mum stopped and said, 'I see you've got Mike's sweater over your shoulders,' and Nina said something about how he'd insisted because she was cold, and Mum said, 'Oh really? Insisted, did he? Well, get this, Nina — I've had it with you. You can't have him, or his son, or even his sweater. In fact, I'll take the sweater right now!' And they started fighting . . . Mum was holding it and pulling; Nina was pulling back. Then suddenly she let go . . . And Mum screamed and disappeared.'

There was a sudden silence, broken only by a seagull's cry. Watching Toby's too-white face, Kirsty swallowed.

'OK, Toby,' said Mike, who had his arms round his son by now. 'It's over now. It's happened and you've remembered it all, but it's over, sweetheart. It's over.'

'So what did you do, Toby?' Kirsty was still standing over Nina, who was saying nothing, just watching out of her cat's eyes.

'I — I hid,' said Toby, his teeth knocking together now. 'I hid in the rocks.' He pointed to a crevasse on the sea side of the path. Kirsty looked at the narrow gap in the rock formation, into which a small child might crawl. He'd have been staring straight down at the cruel grey waves as they swirled beneath him. No wonder he'd freaked out on the diving board.

'I saw Nina look over the cliff and call out a couple of times. Then she called out for me, but I stayed quiet and didn't answer. Then it rained harder and she went on down the path. I must have come out then, because I remember looking over through the rocks and at the sea. It had been blue, but it was grey now. I was looking for Mummy, but I couldn't see her.'

At the word 'Mummy', Kirsty saw a shadow of pain cross Mike's face, but he held firmly to Toby's shoulders and didn't interrupt him.

'I kept looking all the way along the top of the cliffs,' Toby continued.

'Wherever I could get between the rocks and look over, I did. But I couldn't find her . . . I kept calling out, but she never answered . . . In the end I found a little space in the rocks and sat there hoping I'd go to sleep and never wake up. I don't remember any more except for Tracey letting me sleep in with Brad, and she slept on the floor next to us, because Dad was at the police station answering questions . . . ' Looking surprised, he stopped. 'They should have asked me the questions, shouldn't they?'

'They did, Toby,' said Mike. 'They did, sweetheart. But when something awful like that happens, sometimes it's best to forget it until you're ready to remember, and that's what happened to you . . . I expect Mummy wanted you to forget it for a while and not remember it until you were older and it would be easier to deal with.'

Well done, Mike, thought Kirsty, wiping away a tear that had arrived from nowhere. She glanced down at

Nina, who was looking scared and sick.

'It was an accident,' Nina said woodenly. 'At first I couldn't believe what had happened. I looked for Toby but couldn't find him. I was going to tell you all, get you to help me find him and get Louise up from where she'd fallen. I knew from the angle of her neck that she was dead. But when I got back to Skinny Point, I lost my nerve. I could see Mike coming down the path, so I waved to Jack, who was just coming in from his swim, and I pretended to go and look for her . . . Then I found Toby wandering . . . He started crying and asking for Louise and I realised he didn't remember what had happened. Then I thought, what difference would it make if I kept quiet? After all, it had been an accident. An awful, bloody accident. No one was meant to die . . . '

'But someone did,' said Kirsty in a cold voice. 'And you took no responsibility for your actions. You ask what difference it would have made? You watched Mike tear himself apart because he couldn't remember his sweater, *the one that was found under his wife's body*, leaving the beach. Toby was riddled with nightmares and doubt. If you can't see what grief you've caused . . . ' Words failed her.

Nina shot her a venomous look. 'You don't think I've suffered . . . am suffering? Why d'you think I come here and throw flowers over . . . ' Blinking rapidly, she looked away at the sea. 'Well anyway, you won't have to put up with me for much longer. Jack's got to go to the States for a while and I'm going with him.' She stared at them defiantly.

Mike was gazing at her with undisguised dislike on his face. 'Don't think I'm going to stop you,' he said. 'Best of luck to you both, Nina. But I don't ever want to see you again . . . Louise was right. I was sorry for you, but Louise always said you were manipulative and had never grown up. Your friendship with her was over long ago. You always wanted everything she had, didn't you? Including me! And, for the record, I was never your boyfriend . . . You made the running and told everyone, including Louise, that I was. You were only ever a friend, Nina, and now I'm wondering even about that.'

Nina attempted to get to her feet. Kirsty pushed her down again. 'No, don't try to get up. I'm a black belt in karate — believe me, you won't get up till I let you . . . There's something else I want to know. There's a little matter of your stalking me over the past month or so, not that I can prove it. But what about when you attacked me just now, what was that all about? Was it another attempt to frighten me off, or was I meant to slip to my death too?'

Uneasily, Nina licked her lips.

'I advise you to leave sooner rather than later, before I think about reporting you to the police for assault.'

Now Nina did look scared. 'You wouldn't!'

'Try me!' said Kirsty.

★　★　★

300

Toby felt somehow lighter than he had ever felt.

It wasn't as though he'd felt particularly heavy before, but now he didn't seem to need to think quite so much or blink quite so much, or even worry about Dad quite so much either. Because now Kirsty was there with them. She'd told him she wasn't about to go anywhere fast — that as long as he wanted her she'd be around to be his friend — and somehow Toby had believed her, which felt pretty cool. She was good at karate too. She'd stretched the truth a bit, she explained, when she'd said she had a black belt, but she'd had lessons. Toby was seriously impressed.

He watched them for a moment or two, his dad and Kirsty. Dad was standing with his arm resting lightly on Kirsty's shoulders. She had her head back looking at him, laughing at something he'd said. It made Toby remember the joke he had to tell her about how to tell the difference between a weasel and a stoat. He'd just ask as though it was a nature question and when she couldn't answer, he'd say, without the flicker of a smile, that a weasel was weasily wecognisable whereas a stoat was stotally different.

She'd laugh, and so would Dad.

Toby felt warm and happy inside.

* * *

It was remarkable, thought Kirsty later, how quickly people could recover.

They were sitting on the beach, relaxing. Toby was running on the sand with the other children, occasionally splashing into the shallows with Buddy barking alongside him. Tracey and Tim had discreetly parked themselves some distance away and were avidly talking together, probably about the revelations that had been made to them when Kirsty, Mike and Toby had arrived back at the house.

Mike was sitting beside her, his face devoid of the closed-in expression she'd come to associate with him; he even had a half smile on his lips. Those lovely lips.

She smiled. Earlier they'd had a long conversation, and for once Mike had held nothing back. He'd told her hesitantly at first, but gradually increasing in confidence, how difficult he'd found it to move on after Louise's death. How he'd always felt it was his fault. That he should have gone with them; that, because of their earlier row, Louise couldn't have been concentrating to stray off the path and so close to the danger zone.

He told her how later, Nina making advances had completely thrown him and made him tighten up on his emotions even more; and then when, not long after that embarrassing episode, the au pair he'd employed to help him with Toby had suddenly wanted to leap into bed with him, he'd become terrified of any woman he found remotely attractive.

'Of course, the moment I set eyes on

you, I knew I fancied you,' he said, his eyes crinkling at the corners. 'But I also thought you were way out of my league . . . You were too young, too pretty and too optimistic to fancy a dull old stick in the mud like me. Then, when I realised you quite liked me too, I was even more terrified. What if I got hurt all over again? What if Toby really formed an attachment to you and you walked out on us? What a wimp I was. I should have just gone for it, shouldn't I?'

Kirsty smiled. How to explain that it was his very seriousness and vulnerability that attracted her in the first place? But she didn't need to explain, she knew that. So now, she put out a hand and stroked his cheek; then, with her finger, she traced the outline of his lips. 'Mike,' she said. 'There's something I've just got to tell you.'

For a moment the old worried look came back into his eyes.

'You have got the most kissable lips I've ever seen in my life.'

He gave a half-laugh and pulled at his ear. 'Shall we put that to the test?' he said.

'I thought you'd never ask,' said Kirsty, leaning towards him.

THE END

We do hope that you have enjoyed reading this large print book.

Did you know that all of our titles are available for purchase?

We publish a wide range of high quality large print books including:
Romances, Mysteries, Classics
General Fiction
Non Fiction and Westerns

Special interest titles available in large print are:
The Little Oxford Dictionary
Music Book, Song Book
Hymn Book, Service Book

Also available from us courtesy of Oxford University Press:
Young Readers' Dictionary
(large print edition)
Young Readers' Thesaurus
(large print edition)

For further information or a free brochure, please contact us at:
Ulverscroft Large Print Books Ltd.,
The Green, Bradgate Road, Anstey,
Leicester, LE7 7FU, England.
Tel: (00 44) **0116 236 4325**
Fax: (00 44) **0116 234 0205**